"Rand, I Can't," Leigh Whispered. "I'm Not Good At This."

"Sure, you are. Everyone is good at a waltz."

His hair was disheveled, his body radiating heat, his shirt open at the throat and his clothes as contemporary as today. But he bowed with courtly charm, her knight, and his gaze shimmered on her like she was a princess dressed for a ball.

The lilting strains of the waltz were unbearably seductive.

Rand smiled, a rogue's smile of satisfaction, and then he whirled her away.

A waltz, Leigh discovered, was not a slow dance at all. Bodies teased, yet only brushed. Hands touched, eyes met and the heart beat faster because it was the nature of a waltz, to seduce the heart.

When the last chords of the music faded, Leigh was breathless and warm and exhilarated, and Rand was . . . close.

Dear Reader:

Welcome to Silhouette Desire! What a month this is, with six sinfully sexy heroes from six sensational countries featured in our *Man of the World* program. You'll be finding out all about these tantalizing men between the covers of six romances written by some of your favorite authors: Linda Lael Miller, Lucy Gordon, Kathleen Korbel, Barbara Faith, Jennifer Greene, and BJ James.

By now I'm sure you've noticed the portraits of our heroes on the covers of each *Man of the World* book. Aren't these hunks handsome? I simply couldn't decide which hero I loved the best, so I decided to just love them all.

And don't miss the special letter from the author in front of each book. These talented women have taken a little extra time to compose some words to you, describing how they chose their hero and his country.

So thrill to the sensuous love stories in *Men of the World*. From the United States to Europe to the hot desert sands, the books are about six heroes you'll never forget. Please don't hesitate to write and tell me what you think of this exciting program *and* of Silhouette Desire. I'm always more than happy to hear from our readers.

I know you'll love *Men of the World*. Happy reading!

Lucia Macro

Senior Editor

JENNIFER GREENE

FALCONER

SILHOUETTE *Desire*®

Published by Silhouette Books New York

America's Publisher of Contemporary Romance

SILHOUETTE BOOKS
300 East 42nd St., New York, N.Y. 10017

FALCONER

Copyright © 1991 by Jennifer Greene

ISBN: 0-373-05671-0

First Silhouette Books printing October 1991

All the characters in this book have no existence
outside the imagination of the author and have
no relation whatsoever to anyone bearing the same
name or names. They are not even distantly
inspired by any individual known or unknown
to the author, and all incidents are pure invention.

Printed in the U.S.A.

JENNIFER GREENE

lives on a centennial farm near Lake Michigan with her husband and two children. Before writing full-time, she worked as a personnel manager, college counselor and teacher.

Ms. Greene has received many awards for her category romances and most recently won a RITA Award from the Romance Writers of America for the Best Short Contemporary Novel of 1989. She was also named Best Series author of 1988-1989 by *Romantic Times*. She has also written as Jeanne Grant.

A Special Letter From Jennifer Greene

Dear Reader:

My setting for *Falconer* came from a summer
I spent in Europe years ago. I never forgot the
country around the Alps—and especially Austria.
It's truly a land of fairy-tale castles and wonderfully
romantic lore.

Like my memories of Austria, the hero in this story
had been lodged in my mind for years, waiting for a
chance for me to write about him. Rand is my
"Bavarian Knight"—both a romantic lover and a
strong, sure man of unshakable values—but he has
an unresolvable problem. He's torn between two
countries—fiercely loyal to his own and yet unable to
walk away from his commitments to another.

Even a strong, sure *Man of the World* can't move
Gibraltar on his own. Rand needs a little help. He
needs a woman. The right woman. So I gave him a
little "sleeping beauty" named Leigh.

I hope you enjoy the story as much as I enjoyed
writing it.

Sincerely,

Jennifer Greene

One

The Irish setter flushed out a covey of quail. Rand quickly released the jesses of the peregrine and hurled her into the air. She spotted the quail, but unfortunately her prey were predator-smart. They sensed her shadow and scurried for cover. A thicket bordered the mountain meadow—the quails' natural home, and impenetrable to the falcon.

"Come on, love. Come on, come on..." Although the meadow was cool, the late-afternoon sun reflecting off the snowy Bavarian mountain peaks was blinding bright. Rand raised his gloved hand to shield his eyes.

His peregrine circled, made her choice, and then dived in a breathless blur of speed and grace. Seeming without effort, her talons extended and captured her prey. "Now bring her home, sweetheart. Come on, come on.... *Damnation*."

Rand lowered his hand and rocked back on his heels with frustration. The falcon *knew* she was supposed to bring him the prey, *knew* she would be rewarded with a far choicer piece of meat than a winter-scrawny old quail. He'd named her Kamikazi because she was the best hunter he'd ever found—fast, fearless, and aggressive. Nothing distracted her; no size of prey intimidated her; she was the fastest raptor he'd ever seen and she could catch anything that moved. Unfortunately—and contrary to all laws of nature—the damn bird freed her prey. She liked to hunt, not kill. She liked to catch, not keep.

Eventually, though, she seemed to remember that she had the best training of any falcon this side of the Atlantic. A textbook study of perfect obedience, she flew back to him and settled with a regal fluff of feathers on his outstretched glove.

Rand retied her jesses and lowered the hood over her head, swearing at her the whole time in a low, lover's croon. "You know how many birds I've worked with? And no one but you ever gave me this kind of grief. You're the bravest beauty I've ever seen in the air, and the worst coward, the absolutely worst, when it comes to reality. You're supposed to *want* to kill them, you dimwit. They're *your* food chain, not mine."

The peregrine had received similar lectures before. Then and now, she ignored them. The only reason Rand wasted his breath was that the hood never calmed her as quickly as the sound of his voice.

He had worked with birds so long that his shoulders and arms were as muscled as iron. Even so, the peregrine felt deadweight heavy by the time he hiked from the far edge of the deserted field to his old BMW on the road. It took some time to get the Irish setter stashed in the back and Kamakazi settled on her perch between the two front seats, her favorite place to ride. Rand didn't climb in himself.

When he first released the falcon, he'd noticed the bright yellow Volkswagen pause and stop at the roadside. From the corner of his eye he'd seen the lone women step out, but his attention, then, had been concentrated on the falcon.

Now he was free to concentrate on her. And he did.

As he ambled toward her, he easily pegged her for an American, not because of the little phrase book she was clutching more desperately than a life buoy, but because of her eyes. Lots of Austrians had blue eyes, but hers were a uniquely clear, true, flag-waving navy blue.

Beneath the pair of navy blues was a spray of freckles—another American giveaway. The freckles were covered discreetly with makeup, but undeniable, and perched on an upturned nose. The nose was cute, but the mouth was wicked. Her lips were soft, sunglossed, shaped to make a man think of kissing, and just a little unsteady. She may have wanted to catch his attention, but the closer he came, the more nervous she got.

"Bitte...."

She glanced up, as if seeking some assurance that Rand understood her. He nodded. Her "please" was a sinful mangle of German pronunciation, but it wasn't tough to figure out she needed help. Slowly he pulled off his glove, flexing the circulation back into his wrist and fingers, feeling a little circulation flex in another part of his body as well.

She was definitely eye-catching...but so nervous. Maybe she was wary of men with beards, but he didn't bite. Flirt, yes. Bite, no—unless, of course, he was asked.

Rand generally aimed to please a woman, whatever her mood. At thirty-five, he'd had his share of successes—and rejections—but to his memory he had never aroused worry in a lady before. At least, not upon first meeting. Not this much worry. Muttering her frustration with the language, she thumbed through her phrase book with frantic speed.

He didn't mind the brief wait. It gave him another chance to enjoy the view from a closer distance.

She was youngish—ballpark thirty, but no more. He checked her left hand for rings and discovered none. Obviously American men were losing it, he thought fleetingly.

She really *was* special. Not beautiful or even striking, but she had a freshness and softness that was its own allure. Her hair was mussed, driving-in-the-wind mussed, and a rich strawberry blond that layered back from her fine-boned face. No mousse, no lacquer, just a breezy natural style that suited her.

She was wearing new boots, good soft leather, that shaped her slim calves and had enough of a heel to bring her up to his nose in height. Kissing height, he thought wickedly...at least while she was wearing those boots.

She should have worn a jacket—the spring's crisp breeze had her shivering—but he was happier she hadn't. A hand-tooled leather belt divided her raspberry blouse from a loose-flowing skirt. The blouse made a delectable dip on her long white throat and silky fabric hugged the curves of her breasts. She was built. Rand had never been obsessed with one particular part of a woman's body, but if he *had* been tempted along those lines...

"Bitte," she repeated more frantically. Rand cocked his head, trying to communicate that he'd probably do anything short of walking on water for her.

The responsive flush skating up her cheeks charmed him. She knew he was looking her over. If it had offended her, he would have stopped. She didn't act offended—or uninterested—but she was certainly becoming more flustered by the second.

"Ich bin... ich bin..." If she fingered through her phrase book any faster, she was going to rip the pages. Eventually she came up with a rushed, *"Ich bin zuckerkrank!"* But almost as quickly her face fell. "Damn." And to him, *"Nein, nein, nein."*

Rand continued to wait patiently, fairly sure she hadn't stopped a stranger on a mountain road to announce that she was a diabetic. It was conceivable that she had a health condition, but he doubted it. Her skin had a vibrant glow, her eyes far too much sparkle.

She tried a second time. *"Ich bin schwanger?"* She looked at him. He gravely shook his head, trying to keep the devil out of his smile. The breeze was blowing her skirt against beautifully rounded hips—and a distinctly flat stomach. Not that she couldn't be expecting, but it was like the diabetes. Somehow it seemed a tad unlikely that she'd accost a total stranger to discuss her pregnancy.

"Well, *ich bin something,*" she said helplessly, and made those pages fly. "I've got it. *Ich bin verloren.* Wouldn't you think I'd have memorized that word by now? *Verloren!*" She looked at him with such hope.

"Yeah, I kind of figured you were lost," he said easily. Even after seven years in Austria, he hadn't lost his Pennsylvania accent. "Where are you trying to get to?"

Discovering he was a fellow American seemed to give her no relief. He didn't doubt her basic intelligence—her eyes were bright and quick—but her tongue was still trying to trip over itself. "I don't... exactly know."

Rand leaned against her ear, cocking a lazy knee forward. "That'll make it a little trickier. Not insurmountable. Just trickier. Although if worse came to worst and you were lost on this mountain all night, I'll bet the two of us could find some interesting way to wile away the hours and keep warm—no? That isn't quite what you had in mind?" She was shaking her head, but finally he'd wooed a startled smile. "We'd have a good time. I promise," he coaxed. She shook her head again, but he won a second smile. The tension in her shoulders eased, just a little. "Well, hell. I suppose there is another alternative or two. You know where you were headed?"

"Yes, of course." She promptly garbled out about a twenty-seven syllable word, all consonants, that presumably was intended to resemble some identifiable location.

"Maybe you could try that one more time?"

She tried. Rand scratched the tickle of dark beard on his chin. Tactfully he ran through all the possibilities he could think of, but unfortunately that was a no-end proposition. Even if he stuck to the Province of Tirol, there were limitless lures to appeal to a tourist—skiing, lakes and mountains, castles and churches and medieval lore and music.

Eventually, when he couldn't pin down her destination, she reached in the open window of her car and brought out a map. Actually, she brought out a dozen of them, all wrinkled, all used, none of which—under the circumstances—were ever going to help.

"I've never had a problem with directions. Ever. It's just this trying to drive on the left side of the road," she explained. "I can't seem to get my bearings."

Rand could see that. For several hours, she had apparently been trying to locate Neuschwantstein, one of the most famous castles in Europe, located just across the West German border near Fussen.

It wasn't tough to find, unless you were headed south instead of north.

"I'll bet you've had a little trouble getting around," he murmured.

"You wouldn't *believe*."

He'd believe. "I'm afraid, this late in the day, that the castle will be closed if you tried to drive the distance now. But next time you get the urge..." Taking a chewed-off pencil from his pocket, he made her his own map. She was no dunce. Eliminate all references to compass readings, and she absorbed the information faster than the speed of sound.

By the time she stashed the makeshift map in her purse, Rand had introduced himself and wooed her first name out of her—Leigh. Not much else. She'd just arrived in Austria; she was here for a month; it appeared she was traveling alone.

She willingly answered his few questions, but only as though she thought it was necessary to humor him, for flirting with her. Rand was captivated, watching her "handle" him...face flushed, trying to match his teasing ways...arms wrapped around her chest, trying to give him every excuse to leave. Shyness and pride. It was a rare combination, and the thought struck him that she wasn't safe let loose. Not alone. She couldn't "handle" a teenage boy, much less a lone wolf who'd been around the block.

Maybe too many blocks, Rand thought dryly...and knew damn well that a true Austrian gentleman would leave her alone.

He had the Austrian blood, but the gentleman genes had been badly diluted. His father's side had always bred flirts. Besides, it was partly her fault he wouldn't let her escape. By then, she'd made the terrible mistake of admitting interest in Kamikazi.

"I was looking for someone to ask directions from, but that isn't really why I stopped," she said hesitantly. "I saw you in the field with the falcon. I was pretty sure it was a peregrine—they're coming back in the U.S., one of the few endangered species success stories, so I've seen dozens of pictures. Only I never expected to see one alive, much less one that was trained to hunt like that— I couldn't look away. It has to be your bird?"

"Not exactly. She's only mine on temporary loan while I'm training her."

"So that's what you do? Work with birds?"

Rand wanted to know about her background, not
bore her with his, but her shyly asked questions at least
kept a conversation flowing. The capsule history was
familiar to anyone who knew him. From the time he
was a kid, he'd never been able to shake his fascina-
tion in falconry. Vet school had been the ticket to
medical training, but the best way to get hands-on experience with birds of prey was to apprentice under a
master falconer. He'd licensed in the U.S. and worked
with a falcon recovery program, training birds on the
side.

"I did that until seven years ago. I had family
here—an Austrian grandfather I'd never met." A
shadow darkened his eyes, but it wasn't for Leigh.
"Anyway...I came here and I stayed. Hunting with
falcons and hawks is hardly new around here—the old
line aristocracy loved the sports for centuries. I found
some interest, started a small avian hospital, and work
with training the birds directly whenever I can."

"So you've been in Austria since..." Rand knew
she'd been interested. It was in her eyes, in the way she
listened, but suddenly she checked herself. "Good
grief, I never meant to pry—or take up so much of
your time—and I'd really better be going. It's getting
so late...."

She hadn't been prying, and there had been nothing about the conversation to suddenly scare her off,
but Rand guessed what had. Lightning struck a sunlit
mountain meadow every time they made eye contact.
He had been seriously talking with her. Not flirting.
Seriously becoming interested in her, not playing a
game. And the just-a-little-dangerous sexual vibra-

tions humming between them were building faster than a mountain storm.

He wasn't alone. An awareness of that sweet electrical sizzle suddenly hit her, too. Only her instantaneous response was to dive into her purse for her car keys.

"You can't leave yet," he insisted.

"I have to." As if she was late for a train, she surged for her car door.

"Hold on there. We only worked on half the puzzle— I know where you were headed, but not where you were trying to get back to." His comment didn't stop her from climbing into her car, but at least it made her pause. She'd forgotten she was lost. "I'm assuming Hautberg?" Considering the road she was on, it was the most logical guess.

"Yes."

"Do you know how to get there?"

"Heavens, yes," she said breezily.

She knew diddly squat. He was thankful for her weakness in geography because it gave them a few more minutes together. Pointing her west instead of east, though, only took so much time. It wasn't enough.

She was a tourist on holiday, he reminded himself. Much more relevant, a wolf didn't prey on lambs—not in Rand's book on ethics—but he still wanted to see her again. It wasn't the sexual tug. Hell, throw any man and woman alone together and some level of chemistry kicked in. Rand had seen too much life, though, not to recognize that a certain draw, a certain magic with a special woman was all too rare.

When she reached out to thank him for his help, her soft palm ignited that almost-dangerous promise of magic all over again. When he didn't immediately release her hand, her cheeks flushed and her eyes flew to his. Lord, those eyes. The word in German was *niedlich*.

Beguiling.

Most reluctantly, he freed her hand and watched her quickly strap herself in. "I'd hate to see you end up in southern Spain the next time you head toward Neuschwantstein. Most afternoons I can steal an hour off." He was getting used to that blond head shake horizontally instead of vertically. "I could bring references. Half the people in Hautberg know me—anyone'll tell you that I have a sterling character. No criminal record, no exciting vices, haven't kidnapped any small children or blondes in years, and by chance, I'm one hell of a navigator." She smiled, but she was still shaking her head. Cocky humor was getting him nowhere, so he dropped it. "I know you don't know me, Leigh. But that really is all I had in mind—sightseeing for an afternoon, maybe dinner, a chance to talk to someone from home. No hidden agenda. Consider it?"

She finally seemed to realize that he was serious. "I . . ." She pushed in the clutch and started the engine before looking at him again. There was willingness in her eyes, a winsome, soft, clear, want-to. Then her lips pressed firmly together. "Thank you. Honestly and for everything. But I don't think so."

So that was that. Rand told himself you couldn't lose something you never had. Hands on his hips, he watched her turn the car around, zip down the road several yards... and then stop.

Seconds passed. Twenty seconds, then thirty, then a full minute.

Slowly, the car backed up to where he was standing. She reached over to crank down the passenger window and said, "*Yes*. If you meant it."

"I meant it. Thursday?"

"All right."

"Noon?"

"All right."

"Maybe you'd like to tell me where you're staying?"

It seemed like a fairly basic question, nothing tricky, nothing scary, but she closed down like a clam shell protecting its pearl. She'd crossed an ocean and traveled several thousand miles—alone—which said something about her courage as well as her spirit of romance and adventure. Getting the bra off his first girl when he was sixteen, though, was a lot easier than getting the name of the inn where Leigh was staying.

Eventually she caved in. Rand watched her car until it disappeared from sight, then took a rueful breath. He hadn't worked that hard for a date since he was a kid.

He hadn't felt this rush of adrenaline since he was a kid, either.

It bothered him. Walking back to his car, he mentally corrected that thought. *She* bothered him. He hadn't imagined the draw between them...but he bore the responsibility for the match he'd just lit. He'd first mistaken Leigh's shyness for what it was—vulnerability.

But she was safe with him, Rand told himself. No one knew a lamb's vulnerability better than a wolf. If Leigh had crossed a continent for a little taste of adventure and romance, he was uniquely qualified to give it to her.

He was also uniquely qualified to insure a relationship went no further than that. Rand had never become a wolf by chance. He was stuck in a country not his own, for an indefinable period of time, bound by circumstances he couldn't change. That made a serious relationship impossible. Which he knew.

And which was why there was absolutely no possibility that he would hurt Leigh.

None.

"Garage" was one of the few signs Leigh could reliably identify. She parked the car, climbed out and headed directly for her Bed and Breakfast inn a block down.

Her boot heels skimmed about a foot and a half above the pavement. Who said you couldn't walk on air? Her stomach growled with hunger, yet she passed the bakery and café without a glance. Who needed food?

Not that she was biased this evening, but Hautberg was unquestionably the most wonderful place on earth. The sun was just setting, the sky behind the mountains on fire. Small shops cluttered the alley-narrow streets with all the charm of medieval times. Homes and shops alike had high peaked gables and mullioned windows and, always, chimney pots of cheerful flowers. Onion-domed churches rose above the town and in the background, never ignorable, were

the mountains fringed with dark firs, the forests as
thick as in the days of castles and knights.

Her step still winged, humming under her breath,
Leigh ducked in the door of the two-story inn, claimed
her key from Frau Stehrer—who looked aggrieved she
didn't stop to chat—and zipped up the stairs to the
first door at the top.

Inside her room she flipped the latch, hurled her
purse and kicked off her boots. Her feet were sore. She
didn't care. The open alcove window let in a frigid
draft of mountain night air. She didn't close it. She
never walked in the room without thinking that medieval maidens had bed chambers like this. The bed's
dark carved headboard stretched as tall as the slanted
ceiling; the feather mattresses were draped with a
white lace counterpane—handmade—and the wooden
plank floor creaked with every step. She loved the
room, but tonight she barely noticed it.

She threw herself on the bed, wrapped her arms
around her chest, and stared at the ceiling with the grin
of a witless goose.

*Has it occurred to you, Merrick, that you're acting
immature and balmy and like a just plain total fool?*

It had. Any second now, she was going to climb
down from the ozone layer and retrieve her common
sense. Not yet.

Fairy tales didn't happen. Not to her. Thirty years
old, and nothing remotely resembling a fairy tale had
ever happened to plain, dowdy, dull old Leigh Merrick. Until this afternoon.

He'd actually seemed to find her. . . attractive.

He'd actually been . . . flirting with her.

Not just anyone. *Him*. And if there was ever a man who sneaked out of a woman's most judiciously buried private fantasies, it was Rand Krieger. Leigh closed her eyes, remembering the moment she'd first caught sight of him. He had been hurling the falcon in the air, his tall, lean body captured in the sun. The bird had soared and he'd watched it, his dark hair blowing in the wind and his strong shoulders braced, looking like a Bavarian warrior or a knight of old.

Maybe he was. If knights didn't look like Rand four centuries ago, they should have. His face was angular, with sharp cheekbones and a hawk's nose. His shock of unruly brown hair was threaded with copper—the same copper that streaked the beard on his chin. The smile of a rogue was tucked in that beard, and the devil should have his eyes. His dark coloring was already striking, but his skin also had the healthy burnish of sun and wind, making his eyes appear even bluer—a startling, arresting, searing blue.

Good looks were only half the package. Leigh had seen his gentleness and affinity with the falcon, heard the dark, subtle change in his voice when he mentioned his grandfather—there were depths to Rand, secrets in the hard-driven character lines on his brow—but he was more than adept at hiding those from a stranger. At least if that stranger were a woman.

When he'd turned the full force of those baby blues and rogue's smile on her, Leigh had kept wanting to look over her shoulder, quite positive there must be another woman standing there...a woman with poise and allure and sex appeal, the kind of woman who would naturally interest him.

Only no one else was there. Leigh opened her eyes, still feeling exhilarated and champagne high, but suddenly a little shaken, too. It was just a game. It wasn't supposed to work. The new clothes. Losing twenty pounds. The makeup that concealed her freckles, the rinse that covered her mousey-dull hair, the bra that pushed up a figure she'd never considered flaunting before, the new haircut—it had never occurred to her that any of it would really work.

She hadn't come to Austria to trick a man—or fool anyone—about the kind of woman she really was.

It was just that back in Stanton, Kansas, her thirtieth birthday had hit her like a submarine, a blitz, a sniper's machine gun, a nasty surprise. There was nothing wrong with her life. There was nothing wrong with being a childrens' librarian—a job she loved—and nothing wrong with a reputation for being reliable and sensible and practical. From her high school days, she'd earned the label of wallflower, and even that hadn't bothered Leigh because she was honestly a wallflower by choice. Some people couldn't stand rats. She couldn't stand being the center of attention, had never shaken a bad case of shyness with strangers.

But then the big 3-0 had hit. And hurt. She didn't want to change her life exactly. She certainly knew better than to believe she could change her basic character. But she could suddenly see that the patterns of her life were the habits of loneliness...and that was the way it was always going to be.

"Accept your lot, gal," her Aunt Matilda had always told her. "You never had the spark to catch a man, and that's just the way it is. Some of us are doomed to be ordinary. You fight it, you'll just make yourself unhappy.''

Leigh had long ''accepted her lot.'' But there had been a wish in her heart when she'd blown out the landmark thirty candles on her birthday cake. She wished that once in her life—just once—she could be someone else. A different kind of woman. Someone...impulsive. Someone daring and exciting and maybe even a tad wild. Someone pretty. Someone fun.

It was a ridiculous, silly wish, but it lingered in her mind and stuck there like taffy. It wasn't impossible—if she went far enough away where no one knew her. Not forever, but for a short time, she didn't have to be staid, dull Leigh Merrick—if she just had the guts to do it.

The pragmatic saving patterns of a lifetime had easily paid for the trip, and Austria had been her natural choice. No one could possibly know her there, and it was her great-grandmother's country. As a child she'd heard countless tales of the mountains and castles and the music. Always the music. From Austria had come the music of Mozart and Haydn, Schubert and Johann Strauss. Strauss, the father of the waltz, and in the history of lovers had there ever been a more romantic dance than the waltz?

So it had to be Austria, but from the time Leigh bought the plane fare and started the diet and begun shopping, it was just a game. The change in clothes and hairstyle was just pretense, part of the fun. She was still Leigh.

She never meant to fool anyone. It had never occurred to her that she could ... much less that for half an hour, in a wonderful sunlit mountain meadow, she would attract the interest of a man like Rand Krieger.

"Gal, you're being a dang fool," Aunt Matilda would have said. "You couldn't hold a man like that. He saw you all dressed up, figured you for a tourist in town, an easy mark. A fast ticket for some free sex. What else could he want from you?"

Leigh suddenly grabbed a pillow and hugged it to her chest. Even five thousand miles away, she couldn't escape the harsh, horse-sense realism that her aunt was famous for. Aunt Matilda would have put it in spades. Leigh didn't know Rand. She'd never been this close to dangerous waters before. She had no reason on earth to believe he wanted anything more than a fast lay, a fling with a stranger. Maybe like his falcon, he'd picked out easy prey.

The Lord forgive her, but maybe she didn't care. Was it so terrible, so unforgivably sinful to like that look in his eyes, to feel good that Rand had noticed her as a woman, maybe even wanted her?

All she had was a month. One short month in her life before she had to go back to being staid, safe, responsible old Leigh Merrick.

Leigh had no illusions. If she gave up this chance, it would never happen again.

Two

Leigh stood in front of the bathroom mirror and started opening tubes and jars. Spread out, there was quite an arsenal.

A cosmetologist had sold her all the war paint. The lady—who'd been on commission, hardly a boon to her credibility—claimed that it was no sweat at all to make freckles disappear, change eye shape, hide shadows, add shadows, make a small mouth look bigger, and fool the whole world into believing that she had high cheekbones.

Leigh believed that like she believed in fairy godmothers.

Ten minutes later she'd done her worst. Closing the last tube, she glanced in the mirror. Outside the door, the floorboards creaked as Frau Stehrer carried linens up the stairs. Sooner or later, she'd want to get in the bathroom to clean. Leigh meant to hurry, but for a moment her gaze froze on her reflection.

Applying makeup wasn't a new thing anymore, but she had so much fun playing with the pots and tubes that maybe she'd never looked before. Really looked.

The changes were more subtle than blatant—no duckling had miraculously turned into a swan—but she honestly looked like someone else. A woman with big, sensual blue eyes, creamy skin, and a mouth tipped up in a private smile. Hair brushed to a fine gloss tumbled onto her shoulders. Her new blouse was valentine-red with black piping—no dowdy grays for this girl—and fit like a silky invitation. She knew men, this woman. She knew sex. She had the confidence to go after a man she really wanted, and more relevant, would know what to do if she got him.

Cripes, Leigh thought frantically. I can't go through with this.

She'd fooled Rand once. She'd never manage to fool him a second time. *Now* she remembered he'd been standing with the sun in his eyes. Sure, she'd gotten him to laugh—but only over her pitiful sense of direction. And yes, she'd ended holding up her share of the conversation—but only when they were talking about his work; how could she *not* be interested in his falcons?

Anybody could fool anybody for half an hour. A complete afternoon and evening was something else. She wouldn't know what to say. She wouldn't know what to do. She'd bore him to death. She could picture it: her telling him about her life in Kansas, his falling asleep at the wheel, snoring from sheer boredom as his car careened over the edge of one of those dreadfully steep mountain roads. They'd both be dead, only he'd be *relieved* and dead.

"Fräulein Merrick, are you going to be long?"

"Coming," Leigh sang out gaily. She scooped the makeup back into her bag and sailed out, but her stomach was pitching acid.

Noon, he'd said. It was ten minutes to. Truthfully, the only reason she'd sustained nerve this far was that she half expected him not to show. Another woman would be offended if a date stood her up. Leigh had taken great comfort from the possibility. Dozens of men had met her and cheerfully forgotten her in the past. Why not Rand?

The obvious "out" occurred to her. Assuming he did show up, she could always hide in her room and claim sudden illness. It was an immature, adolescent ploy, but hell. It worked for adolescents.

The moment she made the decision, her stomach settled down. She put away her makeup bag and pushed off her shoes—she wasn't going to need shoes if she wasn't going anywhere—and crossed to the window.

Below, the café was open with its outside trestle tables. It was a house of sin, that café. They served *blätterteiggebäck* and *pfannkuchen* and *teegeback*— from the first day, Leigh had discovered that everything irresistible in German was unpronounceable. You didn't have to eat any of the pastries. Just smell them and five pounds would vicariously fly to your fanny. At least her fanny.

She frowned. Pastries, and her recent denial of them, had gotten her into this mess. It was losing weight and experimenting with makeup that had started her believing she could be someone else. Vanity, Aunt Matilda had tirelessly lectured, was the sin of false pride and led to nothing but trouble.

Leigh could still remember the harsh washcloth rubbing off her first experiments with eye shadow, could still hear her aunt's shaming scold. Did she *really* want the boys to look at her? Did she *really* want them to think she was the kind of girl who was easily kissed, willingly led into a back seat, interested in all those terrible things that were always on boys' minds?

As a teenage girl, she sure did and she sure had. Leigh got the message about the wages of sin, but those wages couldn't possibly be more painful than sitting home every Friday night.

She never bucked her aunt, though. Not about makeup, not about anything. She'd spent six months in a foster home after her parents died; Aunt Matilda had sprung her from that horrible place and Leigh never forgot. In later years she had other choices, but somehow habits were easier to keep than change. It wasn't as if she was ever bored. She had her career, community work, her place to caretake. Patterns had hardened into cement before she noticed. Or maybe she had noticed, but taking a risk was, after all, risky.

Come on, Merrick. Put it in black-and-white. You've been a gutless wonder your whole life. You're so scared he'll discover the real Leigh that you've ignored the only thing that should matter. Do you or don't you want to be with him?

Minutes ticked by. Silence ticked with it, until she heard Frau Stehrer calling up the stairs.

"Fräulein Merrick? Herr Krieger is downstairs to see you."

She sprang to her feet, as if someone had lit a match under her heels. Grabbing her purse, she jammed her feet back into shoes, whisked some scent on her throat, and flew down the stairs with, she hoped, her most sophisticated and casual smile.

Gutless Wonder was left home. The Pretend Leigh was on.

Frau Stehrer was filling him in on town gossip when Rand saw her coming down the stairs. The past three days had been hellish—a new glitch in the battle of hospital finances, a poisoned gyrfalcon that hadn't made it, and the ongoing and increasingly serious challenge of handling his grandfather.

Problems weren't going to kill him—he'd handled worse—but Leigh would never know how much she'd been on his mind. He needed this afternoon. And even more than he needed to play hooky, he needed someone to play hooky with—someone so distracting that he forgot pressures and stress, someone so disarming that the rest of the world tuned out when he was with her.

Leigh had affected him like a drench of spring rain. It wouldn't be the same today, he warned himself.

But it was. As she climbed down the stairs, he saw her legs first, then a calf-length black skirt and matching red blouse with black piping. The outfit was striking, feminine, and tasteful, but unless Rand was mistaken, there was a price tag bobbing from the back of her collar. And her slim white hand was clutching a leather purse in a death grip.

She had to climb down two more stairs before he saw the rest of her. Her hair was worn loose, a touchably soft, sun-streaked gold, and she'd tried again to cover up the freckles on her nose. He liked the freckles; he liked the quick, bright eyes. Her chin was locked in a stubborn, determined line—no way *she* was afraid of meeting the devil—and her lips were tipped in a brazen, radiant, dare-the-world smile that was just the tiniest bit . . . shaky.

When their eyes met, he saw a swallow catch in the pulse of her throat. Rand was leaning against Frau Stehrer's check-in counter. He should have immediately straightened, greeted her, put her at ease. But for that spare second, a tornado couldn't have budged him.

He remembered her nervousness. It would have bothered him if her nerves were a symptom of fear, but Rand didn't buy that. Leigh wouldn't have shown up if she were scared. She wouldn't have dressed for him, fussing with the details like fresh perfume and just-brushed hair, for a man she wanted to avoid. The flush on her face was less a blush than simply color. The color of heat, excitement. She was that strongly, sexually aware of him as a man.

Rand could neither reason nor explain it—in a thousand ways, she was unlike any other woman he knew—but he felt the same compelling draw. Their eyes were still locked when Frau Stehrer looked at both of them and muttered something quick in German.

Leigh obviously didn't understand. Rand straightened from the counter and deliberately strode toward her. "She said to have you back by midnight, or she'll call out the equivalent of the Austrian Mounties. You must know Greta by now—she takes on every boarder like they're one of her children." He reached around her back, and pinched the price tag off her blouse before she could be embarrassed by it. Leigh turned her head, but by then there was nothing to see. He distracted her when he reached for her hand, captured it. As he could have guessed, her palm was as chill as ice, the fingers damp. "For the record, Leigh—"

"Yes?"

"There are no Austrian Mounties."

Nerves or not, she had her share of pluck. "No one to rescue lost maidens in the mountains?"

"Nope."

"Luckily..." She didn't seem to mind his dragging her away from her self-imposed chaperon on a fast track outside. "I'm with you. And I believe you told me you had references in this town to rival a priest's."

"I told you that I had a sterling character," Rand agreed. "Which I did. Until I saw you walking down the stairs. And then I decided there's no reason on earth you should be any safer than you want to be. You'd tempt a saint this morning, Ms. Merrick, so God knows what you'd do to a man under an Austrian full moon—which I understand is in the forecast for tonight."

"I'll be home by then."

"Not if I have anything to say about it."

"If you're not going to behave—"

"I'm not."

"I don't believe we're having this conversation."

"Neither do I. But you're going to have to stop laughing if you don't want to encourage me—hold on, there. This is the chariot. Or it might at least pass for a lady's chariot if I'd remember to do something with all the miscellaneous paraphernalia." He opened the passenger door to his BMW and scooped the wooden bird perch, three leads, and a week's worth of forgotten mail to the back seat. "Just because I forgot to clean the car, don't think I didn't plan your seduction down to the last detail."

"I'm sure," she said wryly.

He handed her into the passenger seat while he mulled the humor in her voice. Leigh had clearly stopped worrying—and began to relax—the moment he started aggressively flirting. The reason was obvious. It never occurred to her to take him seriously. Apparently the idea of her tempting a man was a joke she didn't mind sharing.

He was tempted to kiss her then and there, good and hard—really good and wake-her-up hard—but Frau Stehrer was smiling at them from the window. In a past life, Frau Stehrer was undoubtedly the town crier. More relevant, Rand didn't want Leigh exposed to a grilling when she returned home that night, so he ignored the impulse to kiss her and closed her door, gentleman fashion.

They were out of town in five minutes, climbing the hills in ten. "There are some ground rules for this outing," Rand warned her.

"Ground rules?"

"Critical, unbreakable ground rules. You don't have a worry in the world this afternoon, and neither do I. No history, no past, no problem—nothing is allowed on the agenda but having a good time. And anyone who breaks those ground rules suffers an automatic penalty," he said severely.

"What kind of penalty?"

"Damned if I know. I haven't thought that far ahead yet, but it'll have to be sexual. If you're going to have a penalty, it might as well be fun." He downshifted going into a steep curve. "We'll make that your job, thinking up the penalty. And while you're thinking that up, maybe you'd better tell me something about this castle we're going to see. I know how to get there, but absolutely nothing about the place."

"You don't want to hear a bunch of mothball-old history," she insisted.

"Sure, I do." Actually he much preferred her concentrating on that penalty, but was willing to settle on anything that started her talking.

She willingly talked, but not—intitially—about history. In good time, they left Hautberg in the valley, passed the farmlands, passed the rolling meadows of clover and wildflowers, and climbed into forest country. In the height of the mountains, the big tall pines were as thick as old secrets and a dark, gloomy green that blocked out sunlight.

They weren't "gloomy" to Leigh. She loved the woods, and she noticed everything from the edelweiss growing wild to a sparrow hawk winging in the distance. He noticed that the wind had ruffled her skirt above her knees, that she had great legs, and that her right foot continued to tap on her imaginary brake. His BMW could probably take the hairpin mountain roads without a driver, but Rand had no chance to reassure her. It took three-quarters of the ride to coax her into talking about her castle, but once she did, it was like controlling a lit powder keg.

There had to be other reasons why Leigh had traveled five thousand miles, but the castle of Neuschwantstein was definitely a major priority. For years, she'd obviously read about the place and loved it with all the enthusiasm of a die-hard hopeless romantic. And instead of the dry history lesson he was expecting, she made him laugh.

It seemed that Ludwig II of Bavaria had built "her" castle about a million years ago, and the guy was into swans. Paintings and murals and walls of swans. "Now don't go thinking he was kinky—"

"You said it, I didn't," Rand murmured dryly.

"The swans came from the old Greek myth—the one where Zeus turned himself into a swan to seduce Leda. *She* was the only kinky one in the piece, because apparently she took to her swan lover in a big way—they had a lot of children together."

"How?" Rand interrupted.

"How?"

"How on earth could a human being do it with a swan?"

"Trickily," Leigh said straight-faced. "The *point* is that all their kids were male, and all the men became knights—Knights of the Holy Grail, who devoted their entire lives to protecting women. Like Lohengrin. You know Wagner's opera about Lohengrin?"

"Not exactly," Rand hedged.

"I understand. It's hard for you to concentrate on opera when you're still fascinated with the problem of how a human being and a swan could...um... conceivably conceive, so to speak." She forged right on, even though he was choking on a chuckle. "Anyway, you'd know that opera if you heard the music. You've heard the wedding march a hundred times at weddings—that's Wagner. That's from Lohengrin, and Ludwig built the whole castle around Lohengrin."

"I was wondering when we were going to get back to Ludwig."

"Actually we're all through with Ludwig and moving on to Walt Disney."

"Walt Disney?"

"He fell in love with Ludwig's castle, used it for the setting in Sleeping Beauty—heavens! Stop the car, Rand, could you?"

He braked and cut the engine, bemused at the unabashed stars in her eyes as she hurriedly unstrapped the safety belt and scrambled out of the car. They weren't there yet. A crow could beeline from the German border to Neuschwantstein fairly quickly, but the steep, switchback roads would inhibit a car for another twenty minutes. Leigh had spotted the view from a high break in the trees.

He climbed out of the car and angled behind her, close, because it was pretty obvious she didn't notice or care that there was a precipitous thousand-foot drop just below. No wind whistled this thick in the forest; no bird song intruded, or maybe all sound stopped just for her at that moment. Heaven knew, she viewed her castle with a lover's eye.

Ivory white spires rose from the background of dark green firs. From the distance, the spires and pinnacles looked as delicate and airy as spun sugar frosting. The castle was set on a river gorge, and a wispy tail of fog added to the illusion that it was a lost place in time. A place where knights and legends and fairy tales really might exist.

At least for her. "It's even more than I imagined, more special than all the pictures I've seen of it," she murmured. "Isn't it wonderful?" She glanced at him, suddenly embarrassed. "I'm sorry. I know I'm being silly about this—"

"You're not being silly." Rand reached out and pushed a strand of hair from her brow. She caught her breath at that slight contact.

He caught his at her so quick, so unwilling responsiveness. She'd brought up the fairy tale of Sleeping Beauty. Someone had dragged him to the movie when he was a boy—fairy tales had been his last interest in life—and the plot was vague in his mind. Something about a girl under a witch's spell, asleep for a hundred years, dependent on a man's kiss to awaken her.

Leigh was like that. Maybe there was no witch in her life, but her mouth, her eyes had a slumberous sensuality with a yearning and passion that no inanimate structure deserved; a lover dreamed that a woman would look at him with those eyes.

She needed a lover, Rand thought.

But not him. Maybe during the drive, he'd become caught up in the oasis that was Leigh. She was fresh and quick and quietly perceptive. Her voice was bell-clear, a restful alto; her sneaky humor was an unexpected present, and she was one of those rare women a man could be himself with.

Still—an afternoon's outing was different than an intimate relationship, and for the latter, Rand had always stuck, ruthlessly, to the new breed of woman. Women of the 90s were open about their sexual needs and reliably assertive about what, when, if, and how they wanted a man. He liked the new breed of women.

He respected them. With them he could be, and was, completely honest about what he could and couldn't offer in a relationship.

That kind of straightforward honesty would never be possible with Leigh. She wasn't the new breed. Whatever her age, she still had stars in her eyes. She reminded him of a time and place that didn't even exist anymore—if it ever had. A time when a man wooed a woman the old way... the dance of two people courting each other through a delicate pursuit, a delectable chase and tease, throw in hearts and flowers— Leigh probably believed in the whole damn thing.

And for the same reason, there was no doubt in Rand's mind that he wouldn't touch her with a tenfoot pole.

"Rand?"

"Hmm?"

"Is something wrong? You've been staring at me like I have a smudge on my nose—"

He tilted his head and leaned down, mentally condemning himself from here to hell, but at just that moment, not caring. It was half her fault. At least half. Leigh raised a curious eyebrow when he leaned closer, but she never moved. Any woman over the age of seventeen could guess when she was about to get kissed.

Not her. She probably thought he was going to wipe a smudge of dirt off her nose—and maybe that was why. It never occurred to her that he intended to kiss her, that he wanted to kiss her, that she could tempt a man beyond all reason to kiss her. She couldn't possibly be that hearts-and-flowers innocent.

But she was.

His lips brushed over hers, whispered, wooed, then settled. He didn't move to touch her, hold her. This wasn't a kiss involving tongues or carnal awareness or anything else that might scare her off. This was just...lips meeting. She tasted sweet. She tasted warm.

Maybe he'd never tasted a woman this sweet, this warm. Maybe he'd never kissed another woman. That's how she made him feel. She went all still, her shoulders taut, her arms hanging motionless as if her whole body had suspended for that moment in time. But her eyes closed. And her face tilted up like an offering, and her small lips moved under his, shyly, willingly, yearningly.

She was soft. She was silk, and too late Rand discovered that it wasn't her innocence that drew him, but her. He never deepened the kiss, although desire, sudden and powerful, streaked through his veins like white fire. Leigh wove spells. Dangerous spells. She could make a man believe that the contact of lips alone was a completeness. She could make a man feel heady and wild and infinitely wanted—and dammit, he hadn't even touched her.

Except for the kiss.

He broke off that kiss and lifted his head. The illusion should have been broken then, the spell easily zapped. Only she raised her eyes and looked at him, her lips still wet, and it was still there. The damn fool sensation that he was a knight and she was his lady, and no one, no man, no man on any of the seven continents was going to touch her but him.

The thought, of course, was ridiculous. So ridiculous that he had to smile. "I think," he murmured, "that you could cause a man an incredible amount of trouble, Ms. Merrick. Terrible trouble. Dangerous trouble."

"Not me."

"Yes, you."

"Likely you were thinking about someone else." Her smile promised him that was okay.

His response was swift and gruff. "I was thinking about you. Just you. Only you." She smiled again, sure he was joking, and Rand exhaled a rough breath. At that precise second, he'd have sold his soul for a locked door and twenty-four straight hours in bed with that fragile ego of hers. There were ways and means to instill sexual confidence in a lover. He'd teach Leigh a thorough awareness of her own sensual powers or die trying.

"Is something wrong?"

"Not a thing, honey." At least nothing that a snowball packed beneath his belt wouldn't cure. The idea of driving confidence into Leigh was an honorable cause. What he'd really like to do to her had zip to do with honor. Rand hadn't been this hard, this fast, this hot, since . . .

Never.

Another time he'd have to think about that. Leigh suddenly seemed to realize that they were standing at the edge of a cliff. The skittery nerves were back in her eyes—not what he wanted at all. He grinned and grabbed her hand. "Come on. We came here to see your castle, didn't we? So let's do it."

Only it wasn't meant to be. Within twenty minutes they arrived at the castle entrance, only to discover that regular tours were canceled. A recent storm had caused structural damage. Repairs were in process, but not completed.

They walked the landscaped grounds, and circled the circumference of her spiraled castle twice. Bulldog fashion, he would have led her around a third time if Leigh hadn't stopped him. "Honestly, it's enough," she assured him. "I wanted to see it and I have. It's no major problem that we couldn't go inside."

The hell it wasn't. Rand couldn't believe he'd been so stupid as not to call first. She loved the place. She'd wanted to see those damn swans.

"It's all right, Rand," she repeated.

"It will be," he agreed, and hooked an arm around her shoulder on the way back to the car. "Touring a castle was the agenda for the afternoon—and still is. We'll have to do Neuschwantstein another time, but not to worry. There's more than one unforgettable *schloss* in this part of the country."

But none that he could think of. Not one. There were dozens of castles strewn around the Bavarian Alps, some ruins, some fancy, but Rand had never spent time playing tourist and discovering them, and this late in the afternoon it would be hit or miss to find something.

"Are you sure?" Leigh insisted. "Honestly, you don't have to do this—"

"Hey, no problem. I have a perfect one in mind." *Krieger, try and shut your mouth, would you?*

"You do? What's the name?"

"It's a surprise," Rand told her. He considered what one of the Leigh's heroes or knights or fairy-tale princes would do now. Punt, he decided. Only he'd already racked his brains, punting, and he was short on the skills it would take to conjure a castle out of thin air.

He was only sure of one thing. He wasn't disappointing Leigh.

"You have to give me a hint," she coaxed.

"No hints," he said severely, and made her laugh.

The drive was longer on the way back, because they passed Hautberg and wound around another set of hills. Leigh said the mountains reminded her of hooded monks, and they had to stop once, when she spotted a pair of swans swimming on a forest lake. She found, he thought glumly, romance in nearly everything. Mountains, swans, and particularly—more was the pity—castles.

By then Rand knew where he was going, and he could taste the acid flavor of a bad idea. Not a little bad idea, but a rotten bad idea and a risky one to boot. If there had been another choice—any other choice— he would have taken it.

He felt Leigh's gaze resting on his face as he took a gravel path off the main road. Thick woods bordered the steep drive, redolent with pine, and a silver, gurgling stream followed the road edge until the firs thinned out and blended with a stand of spring-green larch. Leigh found the setting magical. She never said it nor had to. It was in her eyes.

"You're going to need some imagination here," he warned her.

"You have to be kidding. This is incredibly beautiful."

"You think so?" He took the last curve, and the house came into sight. Perched on the crest of a hill, the stone structure sprawled three tall stories. Late-afternoon sun reflected off the bell tower, the gleaming mullioned windows, the ancient carved wooden doors.

The sweep of lawn was velvet green, but the terraced gardens in back were long overgrown. Ivy, probably older than Rand, climbed the house and covered the windows. The house and external buildings looked a thousand times better than they had seven years ago. Even so, they needed work. Possibly the landscaper was lazy. Possibly the landscaper had a few other critical priorities.

Possibly the landscaper, this particular afternoon, had been playing hooky.

Rand stopped the car and turned the key without getting out. "In the fifteenth century, there was a moat around it. And castle walls, a foot thick. Inside, there was once a whole mini city—a granary and bailey, a gate house and armory, the whole bit. There—" he motioned with his hand to the low stone building behind the main house "—was where they originally raised falcons—"

"Falcons?" Leigh took a breath. "Where are we, Rand?"

He pushed a hand through his hair and sighed, heavily and with humor. "My grandfather likes to say that there is an essential difference between the German and Austrian character. Stuck in a hot seat, a German would say that the situation is serious, but not hopeless. An Austrian would always say that the situation is hopeless—but not serious."

"I don't understand."

"It means that we're going to make this work, in spite of a few odds against us. Welcome to my home, Leigh."

Climbing out of the car, he crossed his fingers. It was possible that his grandfather was gone. Thursday night he generally played a game of wattle with his cronies, but it wasn't that late yet.

The problem wasn't whether his grandfather was home.

It was whether Rand could count on him to behave.

Three

———

The instant Rand opened the door, Leigh's ears suffered a deafening assault. There was no live symphony orchestra just inside the black-and-white marble foyer, but it sounded like there was. It also sounded like Mahler. The chords were dark, stormy, turbulent—unbeatable mood music for wars and funerals. Particularly played at this ear-shattering volume.

"Heavens," Leigh murmured.

"You don't like Mahler?"

Walking into someone's house who obviously did, Leigh could hardly be honest. "He's all right."

"I always thought he was all right, too—for anyone in the frame of mind to jump off a cliff. Believe it or not, my grandfather finds him relaxing." Rand squeezed her hand, then let her go. "I'll be right back.

It'll just take me a minute to turn it down and find him— I assume the tape is on so loud because he was trying to hear it from outside. Leigh?''

She was listening. Or trying to above the crash of cymbals.

"My grandfather..." Rand hesitated. He looked at her as if he wanted to say something serious, but the obnoxious noise level seemed to change his mind. He shook his head, and then motioned again that he'd be right back.

When he disappeared from sight, Leigh tucked her arms around her waist and exhaled a long, slow, coward's sigh of relief. So his grandfather was here. They weren't alone. She had been gulping in huge lungfuls of air from the moment she realized Rand had brought her to his place. It was one thing to spend time with a man in a car, and another to be in his house. Alone with him. With the privacy of night coming on. After sharing a kiss that had knocked her socks off.

Glancing around, Leigh mused that if that kiss had been any more potent, she'd probably have stripped him and seduced him right in the woods. Her. Leigh Merrick. The same woman who got hiccups the last time a man had kissed her—Joe Singleton, who ran the dry goods store in Stanton; that date was *not* an experience she enjoyed remembering.

Hiccups had not been her problem with Rand. A potential heart attack, maybe. A serious weakness in her knees, a champagne dizzy fizzy high, a soft pounding in her heart that had been as powerful as a dream, as alluring as the man who caused it...good Lord, that man could kiss.

That's it. Treat it lightly, Merrick. Leigh rubbed her
damp palms on her skirt, feeling way over her head
and not "light" about anything. The kiss had unnerved her, but the man unnerved her more. All afternoon she'd felt good with him, natural, easy. And
all afternoon the niggling thought kept sneaking into
her conscience that Rand hadn't been relating to *her*,
the real Leigh, but the imposter in a new set of clothes,
the faker whose hair color wasn't even honest.

Abruptly the blaring music stopped. She put her
conscience temporarily to bed and concentrated on her
surroundings. Past the foyer was a huge stone staircase, split in two parts, wide enough for six adults to
climb at the same time. Rooms led off double arched
doors on both sides of the hall.

Rand had promised her a castle, Leigh mused, but
this old monster had far sneakier magic than fairy-tale
whimsy. The worn banister, the scuffed black and
white tiles, the drift of lace curtains on the stairway
landing . . . people had lived here, loved here, watched
their children born here over the generations. Maybe
it was a formidably enduring fortress, but it was also
a home.

Only one set of doors were open off the hall, where
she peeked, and then cautiously wandered in. The
huge room had vaulted ceilings and a scent of pipe
smoke in the air. Old damask draperies hung from tall,
narrow windows; papers covered a writing desk; a
massive wood-burning tile stove took up one corner,
cold now—but the room wasn't.

In every corner there were touches of warmth and
color. The furniture looked newer than antique, but a
settee was upholstered in a soft woman's rose.

Thoughtfully Leigh fingered a white wool afghan, beautifully crocheted. Books in German crammed the bookcase, the bindings cracked from use. A mirrored tray displayed a fragile collection of marble eggs in jade, onyx, and pink quartz. She saw an old man's walking stick, obviously in its favored place by the stove, and the worn mahogany table in the front window was covered with a feminine cache of music boxes—at least a dozen, each handcrafted and unique.

The whole room was so lovely that she didn't first recognize what jarred her. There was nothing here of Rand's beyond some books and papers on the desk. Expendable things. It was as if he didn't live here but was only visiting.

Seven years is hardly just visiting, Leigh. But she traced a fingertip on a dusty music box, feeling unsettled again. Rand exuded a sexy, easy confidence that skillfully masked any problems he might have. There were just a few tick-tiny clues that he wasn't happy here—like his lack of things around the house, like the rare shadow darkening his eyes, as if something drove him, rode him hard.

Of course, it wasn't her business—or her right—to care.

Digging her hands into her skirt pockets, Leigh drew back her head and closed her eyes. All day, she'd been euphoric. Wildly happy to be with him, shaken by magic when he kissed her, living out a dream that she'd never expected to become real.

Only the whole stupid dream was starting to feel like an albatross. It was never in her nature to lie to herself or anyone else. She wanted to start over and be honest with Rand—and the Lord knew that option was still open. All she had to do was find the nearest powder room, scrub off the makeup, and when Rand came in, start talking like who she was—a pudgy, unworldly librarian from Kansas who kept cats.

Unfortunately the same reasons she desperately wanted to be honest were the same reasons she couldn't. Rand was more than the sassy flirt she'd first thought. He wasn't a fast stop on the A train. He had a lot of Prince Charming in him—heaven knew, he could give lessons to the devil on beguiling a woman—but he wasn't a dream.

He was a very real man. Rand had taken his own road—and definitely the one less traveled—implying strength of will, determination, courage. But also loneliness. He had a streak of old-fashioned honor, a wicked sense of humor, and he could tease without mercy—but he also took care of a woman, protectively and automatically.

What it all added up to was that she liked him. Not like a dream, not like some trumped-up stupid fantasy or imagination in her head. Leigh simply and honestly liked him. Terribly much.

And she simply and honestly didn't want him to think she was a frump, because God forgive her, he seemed to like her, too.

The distant sound of a rasping cough startled her thoughts—and didn't do a bad job of scaring the wits out of her, either. At the far end of the room, one of the external doors was ajar—letting in air, Leigh had assumed. She had no idea anyone was on the terraced lawn.

Hesitantly she crossed the room, wary of intruding on a stranger, but Rand was still gone. She assumed he was searching for his grandfather, when possibly the older man had been here all the time. So she glanced outside.

The polite smile on her lips froze in shock. An old man was sitting on a stool, hunched over a telescope pointed to the hills. She knew he was Rand's grandfather. His hair was as white as sugar, pinning down his age, and the tall lean build and aristocratic bone structure gave away the Krieger family relationship. It wasn't his looks that shook Leigh, but his clothes.

She recognized the coat with dark piping, the tall black boots. The formal Austrian military uniform was familiar because she saw it every year, specifically on Christopher Plummer in the annual rerun of *The Sound of Music*. Only this wasn't a costume from a movie set, but the real thing.

Unsure what she was getting into, she decided to duck out quickly and find Rand. Only at just that moment, the old man turned his head and spotted her.

He rasped something in German. She shook her head. "I'm sorry, I don't speak the language. *Ich bin*..." Unfortunately there were a zillion *"ich bins"* in her phrase book; there was no way she could remember them all. *"Ich bin* with Rand. And *ich bin verloren,* too. Honestly, I never meant to disturb you. *Bitte* excuse me. I'm terribly sorry—"

He looked like a commanding Bavarian warrior, but he was chuckling when he stood up. "Not to panic so much, *fräulein.* I speak the English." He strode toward her, leathered hands extended to hers in greeting. "I am Theodor Krieger, Rand's grandfather. And you are—"

"Leigh. Leigh Merrick." Her pulse gradually slowed. There was no question the old gentleman had a little problem with reality. The uniform was impossible to ignore, and his focus was disconcertingly vague. Still, she felt the stir of compassion, not fear. The big hands enfolding hers were less than steady. His age was as apparent as his pride and courtly manners, and Leigh knew precisely where Rand had inherited his rogue's smile.

"I'm honored to meet you, Fräulein Merrick. When I heard the music turn off, I knew Rand was home— but I had no idea he was bringing home a guest. Come sit with me."

She wasn't sure that was a good idea. "I believe Rand is looking for you—"

"And he will find me. He always does." He released her hands, but not before he'd studied her thoroughly. "Renate will love you."

"Renate?"

"My wife. She is upstairs dressing. She takes forever," Theodor confessed as he dusted off a white iron patio chair for her to sit in. "We have three boys, you know. Wilhem, Rand, Franz. Wilhem is already twelve. They're growing so fast . . ."

Confused, Leigh tried to fathom how he could have a twelve-year-old son—then abruptly realized that he was caught between the past and present. Again, her heart stirred.

"I was just keeping watch." He motioned to the telescope.

"Watch?"

"For the Nazis, of course."

Leigh's gaze riveted to the old man's face. "Of course," she said gently.

"They're all over Austria, but they have not taken over. Not yet. Not ever. Austrian history is a story of people who have lost everything, time and time again—through plague and seige, famine and politics. The Third Reich is barely an annoying bug by comparison. We will never fall. This is my homeland, my home—my wife and three sons are here. There is no way anyone is taking my home from me."

Leigh had no idea what had happened to him during the Second World War, but he was breaking her heart.

"You are completely safe here," he assured her.

"I'm sure I am."

"I have taken precautions of all kinds. Hoarding food in the cellars for one." The old man hesitated, his brilliant blue eyes suddenly blurred in confusion. "It might be better not to mention that to Rand. He doesn't know. He doesn't understand that we must take them seriously if we are to protect ourselves. Can you keep that secret for me, *fräulein?*"

"I would probably keep any secret you asked me— if you'd call me Leigh."

His lined face creased in a smile. "Then enough of war, Leigh. A beautiful woman doesn't want to talk all the time about war. Rand has shown you his falcons?"

Leigh wasn't sure which Rand he meant—apparently father and son had the same name—but it hardly mattered. "There hasn't been time."

"Kriegers have raised falcons on this land for centuries—I am a falconer myself—but Rand has a true gift with wild creatures. Particularly beautiful, wild creatures. It takes enormous patience and time to win a falcon's heart. Sometimes I think that is the most dangerous quality in Rand—his patience. Watch out, my dear."

"I beg your pardon?"

"Perhaps my English is not so good. I was trying to make a metaphor, but no matter. If my language skills are rusty, my manners are certainly better than my grandson's. And since Rand is being so remiss as to neglect you, I would like to offer to show you the *schloss.*" He rose from his chair and offered his arm, confiding, "I would guess, by now, that he is frantic about finding me. But we will elude him a little longer."

He showed her hidden staircases and family portraits and wonderful old rooms—a nursery, a school room, a hideaway library on the third floor. Although most of the bedrooms were closed off, she caught a peek of Rand's and it made a lump form in her throat. A white doctor's jacket draped a chair, but the rest was neat to a fault. The huge bed was made, no creases. No pocket of change dropped on the bureau, no clutter, no comforts, and like downstairs, there was no sign of personal possessions.

Something was wrong, for Rand, with Rand—but Leigh's host gave her no time to dwell on it. As fascinating as the old house, her tour guide harnessed all her attention. If she was terrified of falling in love with one Krieger, this one she willingly gave her heart to. Theodor's posture was perfect, his step frail. He was terribly confused—his conversation bounced between past and present, always coming back to the upcom-

ing "war"—yet his values emerged clear and strong.
He loved his home. He loved his sons. And more than
anything on this earth, he loved his wife.

They ended up back downstairs, in the farthest
room off the right in the hall. Theodor had to dig a
key from his pocket to open the double doors. Inside
was a massive empty room. Two dusty crystal chan-
deliers hung from the ceiling; marble fireplaces dom-
inated each end of the room; windowed doors led out
to a patio. The glass panes hadn't been washed in
years. Their steps made footprints.

"Renate," he told her, "has balls in here. She loves
music. Haydn, Mozart, gypsy music, even the Heurigen songs of the taverns—it doesn't matter. She loves
it all." He looked down from his great height, patted
Leigh's arm. "This has to be another secret between
us."

"Secret?"

"Rand locked it off. I am not supposed to have a
key. He thinks this room makes me . . . remember too
much. He thinks that it makes it harder for me, but he
is wrong. When I walk in here, I can start to hear
it. . . ."

"Hear?"

"Can't you hear it? The Viennese Waltz? There are
a hundred waltzes, but not like that one. Not for my
Renate. Too much rock and roll, this generation."

By then, Leigh was no longer surprised by his un-
accountable jumps from present to past. "I agree,"
she murmured.

"If you have never danced the old way, the old
waltzes—"

"Maybe you could leave that for me to teach her, Gramps."

Theodor's head jerked toward the door at the same time Leigh's did.

She heard the laidback drawl, and she saw Rand sauntering toward her at his own easy pace. It never occurred to her that anything was wrong until their eyes connected.

He searched her face with such hard intensity that her stomach contracted with nerves—and the most primitive kind of awareness. She'd never seen Rand without control; now she had a glimpse of the stark male fires he kept banked. There was nothing blatant, nothing his grandfather seemed to notice. But Leigh did. He'd shoveled a hand through his coppery dark hair not long ago; his lungs were still out of breath; his shoulders were coiled tense. Her falconer had been badly worried. In fact, her falconer was just plain rattled.

Until she smiled at him.

An hour later, Rand waved his grandfather off. As soon as Theodor climbed into the gray Volvo, Struber and Weinbach—his card-playing cronies—began bickering over the stakes for their game of wattle. They had an identical argument every Thursday night. Grandfather was now wearing a normal pair of trousers, thick sweater and jacket—thanks to Leigh, who had gently suggested that it might not be "safe" for him to wear his uniform in public "in these troubled times."

As the car sped down the driveway, Rand climbed the porch steps back to Leigh. The sun had dropped between mountain peaks, hovering there like a big fourteen-carat gold ball, but it would fall in seconds now. Night always dropped fast in the mountains. Chitchatting with the old man, Leigh had started to shiver and was still shivering, her shoulders hunched and her arms wrapped around her waist. The wind was playing havoc with her hair and for a moment Rand just looked at her, bemused.

"What?" she demanded.

"I just don't believe you, that's what." Playfully cuffing her neck, he hauled her back inside the house. "For the record...if I had known my grandfather was going to be in one of his 'moods' I wouldn't have brought you here. He isn't like that all the time."

"There was no problem," she said honestly.

There was for Rand. The moment he heard Mahler playing, he knew bringing her here was an impulsive risk he should never have taken. He'd searched the property from stem to stern for his grandfather, frantic to find him before Leigh was exposed. He was afraid she'd be frightened. He was going to shoot himself if she were frightened, and Rand knew damn well that Theodor Krieger, in full officer's regalia, when he really got going about the war, could be one intimidating handful to deal with.

But when he'd walked into that ballroom, Leigh had been relaxed, smiling, with laughter in her eyes...and Gramps, of all things, had been flirting with her. He should have known, Rand told himself. He should have known she would be sensitive to a fragile old man—because she was sensitive about everything else.

"Come on, you. We'll build a fire to take off some of the chill. You're still shivering."

He pushed two wing chairs close to the wood-burning tile stove. Leigh curled up in one of them, while he stacked logs and kindling. When he flicked the match, the flames caught with a little whoosh.

The fire would toast her in time, but she wasn't used to the volatile temperature changes in the mountains. He folded her fingers around a shot glass before sprawling in the opposite chair. In the increasingly shadowed room, the fire glow made an oasis of light that made her eyes look midnight blue and illuminated her thoughtful expression.

Given the option, he'd have scooped her onto his lap and kissed her senseless. It felt good to be with her. Too good. So good that he wanted to test exactly how and why Leigh managed to affect him so strongly in this short a time. Unfortunately he just had the feeling she had a slightly different agenda in mind.

"If you're willing to . . . tell me about him, Rand."

"My grandfather?" Pushing off his boots, he cocked a foot on an ottoman. Hell, he knew it was coming. And he could hardly deny the questions in her eyes when he'd made his own bed by bringing her here.

"If it bothers you to talk about him—"

"No, it's okay." He didn't mind telling her, but he was determine to keep the story light and short. Where he grew up, a man didn't push his emotional baggage on a woman. "Gramps was fine until my grandmother died seven years ago. Or I assume he was fine. I'd never met either of my grandparents—my dad used to come over every few years, but the family budget never extended to the whole crew making trips to Europe. Anyway, a neighbor wrote my father, telling him that Gramps was basically . . . losing it." Rand shrugged. "So I came. My father would have—he wanted to—but no one knew what we were getting into, how long it would take to resolve. I didn't have a wife or kids, so I was the logical member of the family to pitch in."

"Then you weren't actually planning on staying here?" Leigh asked.

"It had to be," Rand said simply. "My grandfather was like you saw him this afternoon. There's no way—none—he'd ever willingly leave here. So to desert him to the care of strangers when his only living family is on another continent?" He shook his head. "Besides, I wanted to know him, be with him. He's an old falconer himself so we share that interest, and you saw the buildings out back. One was easy to convert into a small hospital—the setup for raising birds of prey was already here, had been for centuries. I could basically do the same work here I was doing at home."

"You make it sound easy. There couldn't have been anything easy about completely changing your life for seven years."

For an instant his gaze seared on her face. Damn you, he thought softly. Her eyes were warm and caring, and her voice could coax the secrets from a stone. Leigh couldn't know that he never, ever, talked about this. No one asked him; no one guessed what hard, tough prices he paid to stay here.

Firmly he deflected the subject away from himself and back to his grandfather. "He isn't always off. He'll go whole days when his mind is as sharp as a tack. Then I'll walk in some mornings, and that music will be on and I'll find him in that uniform again.

The time he's living out is sometime around 1937, before the Germans occupied Austria."

"Do you know what happened during the war?"

"To a point." He let a sip of aquavitae linger on his tongue until it stung. "My grandfather was around thirty about then, with three young sons. I gather he didn't believe Austria would fall, refused to believe it could happen...and then the chance to get out, for all of them, was gone. The *schloss* was occupied during the war, Gramps was sent to Germany, separated from the family. He lost two sons to illness, and never knew until the war was over."

"Oh, how hard," Leigh murmured.

He nodded. "The European perspective is different than ours. You can't live here very long without getting a picture of how hard those times really were for everyone. By the time Gramps came home, there was almost nothing left. Anything of value inside had disappeared—silver, paintings, even furniture. They had no money. No one did then, and it was simply a different world—the time of old aristocracy and rich landowners was long gone. The way of life they used to know no longer existed."

Rand lifted his hand in a helpless gesture. "I tell myself that I understand why my grandfather slips back to those prewar years, but I really don't. They survived the damn war, eventually made a good living off the land again. They lived together another forty years, as my father tells it, more than happily. He adored my grandmother. So all I can think of was that maybe that was part of it. When his Renate died, the only one who really sustained him was gone."

She said quietly, "Doctors haven't helped."

She didn't phrase it like a question. It was as if she knew he'd pursued that avenue from here to exhaustion. "I could drug him when he gets confused," Rand said dryly. "That seems to be the universal medical solution when a patient is his age. We tried it. I'm not doing it to him again. Anyway, it's not as rough going as I've made it sound. He's not physically ill, he's not unhappy. It's all worked out as well as it can be."

"For him, I can see that. But for you..." She crossed and then uncrossed her legs, then took a breath. "Look, I know it sounds presumptuous coming from someone who barely knows you, but you're honestly not alone."

"Alone?"

Until that moment she hadn't touched the shot glass. Now she took a sip. Just one. Kind of a lunging gulp. "I have an aunt," she confessed. "Actually she's a great aunt—my grandmother's sister. My parents died when I was a kid. At the time I had a couple of uncles, a cousin—anyway, she was the only one who could take me in. She's always been a character. The kids in the neighborhood used to call her 'the dragon lady' behind her back."

"Honey, if you don't like aquavitae, you should have said so. I can get you something else—"

"Heavens, I like it fine." To prove it, she immediately took another bracing sip. Rand could see how she liked it. She calmly smiled at him through a rainbow glaze, and it took a minute for the fire and smoke to clear out of her voice. "Anyway... I think something happened to her a long time ago. A love affair gone wrong, a man who ran out on her. Whatever the story, by the time I came to live with her, she was a classic stereotype of an old spinster, rigid and unyielding. Not that she had much effect on my life—"

"No?"

"Not at all. I had wonderful memories of my parents, and besides, I always understood she was unhappy—"

Rand couldn't take his eyes off her face. "She was cruel to you?"

Her cheeks flushed with embarrassment. "The specifics about my aunt don't make any difference. I only brought her up to tell you that I understand what it's like, to have a relative who can be...difficult to handle. Even if you love them. Even if you've tried your best. Even if you've done everything you know how to do."

Rand nodded. He understood...more, perhaps, than Leigh intended him to. Her nature was to offer comfort and compassion to someone with a problem. Even if it took her two punishing gulps of aquavitae to risk having her kindness rejected.

Somehow, Rand mused, he wasn't surprised to learn about the witch in her background. There always had to be something. Her wary pride, her nerves, her complete unawareness of her own desirability—no woman was a sleeping beauty at her age without a reason.

"Hey," he said softly. She looked up. Lord, those sensitive eyes...and she was hunched forward, clearly prepared to listen to his problems all night. That wasn't why he'd brought her here. The agenda was to show her a castle—and to play knight errant to a shy princess. He was screwing up on all fronts.

He slapped both knees and stood up. "We've been getting serious here. Too serious. Did I or didn't I warn you that there would be a penalty if either one of us got serious about *anything* this afternoon?"

"You did." Jeez, hours had passed. Leigh had prayed in four religions for him to forget that "penalty."

"And it was your job to think up something appropriately wicked to fit the crime," he reminded her ruthlessly.

"I don't remember that part about the 'wicked.'"

"Meaning that you haven't even tried to think one up. Well, I'll give you through dinner, and then you forfeit to my greater—and far more evil—imagination. Now are you a little hungry or a lot hungry?"

Leigh was breathless by the time they sat down at the table. The kitchen was as big as a cavern, all greens and whites, with hanging pots over an old stove and a mammoth pine table—she'd have noticed more if she had a chance.

She was being manipulated, she thought. And by a master with a few archaic ideas about women. She'd learned of Rand's feelings with loyalty, honor and commitment when he talked about his grandfather, but apparently a woman wasn't supposed to be bored with that dull stuff. A woman was supposed to be entertained. She should not be troubled, not be bothered, and certainly not be worried by such mundane details as what on earth he was going to feed her for dinner.

He'd never planned on dinner at his house—which Leigh knew. The pickings were a little slim—which bothered her even less. The cook, though, seemed to think she didn't notice all his subtle, sneaky efforts to keep her happy.

Leigh noticed, but by then she understood how much stress he absorbed with the problems of his grandfather. He didn't need more. Maybe because both of them needed to laugh, neither had to work that hard to make it happen.

Rand was the one who mercilessly turned the meal into a language lesson. *"Käse,"* he told her when she lifted a wedge of cheese.

"Käse," she repeated, in that bell-clear, incredibly mangled accent of hers. "And this?"

"Roggenbrot. Rye bread, made the old way with rye flour and caraway seeds and just a little beer. The French like to throw a little wine in their stews. The Austrians are more inclined to throw a little beer in just about everything. To shorten it up, though—plain old *brot* is bread."

"Brot. That's easy enough. And what are we drinking?"

He chuckled even before he told her. *"Gebirgler fruhschoppen."*

"You set me up," she accused him.

"Come on, try."

She tried three times to pronounce the phrase before giving up with a laugh. "What is it in English?"

"The locals call it something like 'a mountaineer's pint.' It's half red wine, half mineral water, with a little sprig of dwarf pine in it to give it a tang. You like it?"

"It's wonderful."

"Now these." He pushed a plate close to her. *"Blätterteiggebäck."*

"That one, I knew," she said morosely. And pronounced it perfectly. He raised his eyebrows. "Austrian pastries have been my downfall since I arrived here."

They were almost his. Rand watched her take a wedge of the *blätterteiggebäck*. The wedge was bite size, no more. She wanted more. The temptation was in her eyes, the hint of pure, uninhibited, unadulterated, sensual, passionate lust. For the pastry.

"Have a little more," he coaxed.

"Can't."

"Sure?"

"Positive," she promised him.

"Well, that's it for you then. If I can't tempt you into eating any more, then it's time." Rand stood up from the table and reached for her hand.

"Time?"

"Time for you to face the music. The penalty, remember? For daring to be serious before dinner. You didn't think I'd forgotten, had you?"

"Rand, I—"

It seemed a good time for her to go home. She'd taken his whole afternoon and evening, and he was probably tired, had things to do. So she told him, but Rand wouldn't listen.

He led her into the old ballroom, then promptly deserted her with stern orders to stay put. By then, night had fallen completely. In spite of the rising full moon outside, the ballroom was shadowed and as black as pitch.

Rand opened the first, second and then the third set of doors leading outside. Night air flushed in, fresh with the scent of pine, and starlight softened the shadows. He disappeared, leaving her standing in the center of the floor, rubbing her arms to dispel her building feeling of nerves.

When he returned, he was juggling two ancient pewter candelabras. He lit both, and set them on the floor at each end of the ballroom. The candles flickered wildly, but they stayed lit. Rand disappeared again while she was staring at those candles, and seconds later she heard the echoing strains of the Viennese Waltz.

He's said nothing as he'd flown around, setting up all this, and he said nothing when he reappeared in the doorway. Her pulse was beating, beating, as he strode toward her.

His hair was disheveled, his body radiating heat, his shirt open at the throat and his clothes as contemporary as today. But he bowed with courtly charm, her knight, and his gaze shimmered on her as if she was a princess dressed for a ball and no one else had better dare claim her this night.

"Rand, I can't," she whispered. "I'm not good at this—"

"Sure, you are. Everyone is good at a waltz. All you have to do is listen and let the music take you." He lifted her left hand to his shoulder and captured her right. "Hum it with me, Leigh," he murmured.

She hummed it because he asked her. And then because she couldn't resist doing so. The room was dark, the luring, lilting strains of the waltz unbearably seductive.

"You hear it? On the inside?" he asked her.

"Yes."

He smiled, a rogue's smile of satisfaction, and then he whirled her away. Inside, past yellow flamed candles and shadows; outside, around a moonlit dusted patio. Leigh could have sworn she heard echoes of other voices in the ballroom, saw the shadows of other lovers whirling by them, tall proud men and women in long white gloves and slippers. Other times, other spring nights, other couples must have hopelessly fallen in love in this ballroom. She enjoyed imagining them, but not for long. This was her dream. Her night.

A true waltz, she discovered, was not a slow dance at all. Bodies teased, yet only brushed. Only hands touched as feet skimmed the floor; only eyes met, daring and dark with promises; and the heart beat faster because it was the nature of a waltz, to seduce the heart.

When the last chords of the music faded, they were in the middle of the floor. She was breathless and warm and exhilarated, and Rand . . . was close. Close enough for her to see the rampant pulse at his throat. He slowly lowered her hand without releasing it. The silence was suddenly intimate, the pale moonlight reflecting on his face. His smile disappeared and his eyes rested on hers, as black and shining as ebony.

She knew he was going to kiss her. Knew it from the look on his face, knew it from the dangerous, delicious race of her heart. But he didn't.

Not then.

Four

Hautberg was asleep by the time Rand drove Leigh back to the inn. His headlights shone through ghostly clouds of fog, the same fog that curled through the empty streets, misting the dark shop windows and making the pavement glisten with a wet wax shine.

"Sleepy?" he asked as he cut the lights and switched off the engine.

"Very much," Leigh murmured. A dutiful lie. Her pulse was still thrumming waltzes, her heart still beating exhilaration. Given any excuse, she could probably walk on air.

Instead of getting out, Rand flicked on the inside car light. "I notice Frau Stehrer left a lamp in the window, but there's no outside light. It might be easier to find your key in here."

Key, her mind echoed blankly. Earth calling Leigh.
The evening was over. It was time to straighten her
posture, climb out of the car, and remember her
manners.

"Rand... I couldn't possibly have had a more
wonderful time. You went to so much trouble...."
Earth found Leigh, but the return to reality was a heck
of a bump. She dived into her leather purse, praying
that this once—please God!—she'd remembered her
key. Her fingers found the smooth tube of a lipstick,
the bristles of a brush, the snap edge of her wallet,
pennies. Pennies had always reproduced in the bottom of her purse. Pity sense didn't reproduce along
with it. If she had to wake Frau Stehrer to let her in,
she was going to die of mortification. "I loved your
house. I definitely fell in love with your grandfather—"

"What time would you like me to pick you up tomorrow?"

He hadn't really asked her that. It was just since
she'd come to Austria—and met him—that she'd lost
her sense of what was real and what was fantasy. Rand
had probably waltzed with a hundred women in that
ballroom. He had probably taken a thousand women
on moonlit walks by the stream near his house. He'd
probably tempted them all with *blätterteiggebäck*.
She'd be crazy to think the evening had been as
unforgettable for him as it had been for her. "Dinner
was wonderful," she said firmly. "So was the drive
this afternoon. And—there, thank heavens!"

Her fingers identified the serrated edge. She
snatched the key and raised it triumphantly to view.
Rand chuckled. He also immediately turned off the

inside car light, making her pupils dilate from the
sudden blackout.

"How does three tomorrow afternoon strike you?"

"I—" She expected him to reach for the door handle. Instead he turned in the seat, lazily, calmly, to face
her. In the silent darkness, he no longer looked like a
nice, safe, courtly knight. Nice, safe, courtly knights
didn't wear leather jackets, didn't scare a woman
senseless the way he looked at her mouth, didn't reach
out to brush a strand of hair from her cheek. Very,
very gently.

"I never had a chance to show you my birds. I'd like
to. I can't get free until around three, and even then I
have a peregrine I need to work with—but I think you
might enjoy seeing that. Say yes, Leigh."

When she didn't immediately answer, his palm
wrapped around her head and he leaned closer. So, she
thought sensibly, he was going to kiss her. No surprise. Everyone ended dates that way. It made for a
nice, neat, natural cut-off point. She had no fear it
would be like the first kiss, because nothing on heaven
or earth could replicate that first kiss. Besides, this
time, she had a practical hold on reality.

"Say yes, Leigh," he whispered again. His voice was
throaty—low and dark. As dark as a dare.

She felt the warmth of his breath, saw his eyelids
shutter down. The first touch of his lips was more a
stroke than a kiss. But they came back.

His beard was wiry, ticklish, a strikingly erotic contrast to his soft, soft mouth. He wanted another taste.
He stole it, slowly, teasingly, and then he took his own
sweet time stealing another that was deeper and more

intimate. A kiss involving tongues. His tongue, and then tentatively, shyly, hers.

It didn't end, that kiss, until she felt taken over, taken under, sweeping dizzy and shivery. Lightning storms had this kind of electricity. The excitement shooting through her pulse was not forced by Rand, not caused by her, but borne from something they brought to each other...something magical and terrifyingly powerful.

Leigh told herself she was nuts. He wasn't vulnerable. He wasn't lonely. He was a thousand years more life-experienced than she was. It was the imposter Leigh who'd sensed a man's need, responded to it, wanted to believe in it. That game had to stop.

Yet when Rand raised his head, his features were suddenly stark, his dark eyes burned on hers and he wasn't smiling. Just a tad, just a hair, he looked like he'd survived being blindsided by a Mack truck.

It was dark, of course. She couldn't see clearly. When her gaze dropped to his mouth, though, she could see with embarrassing clarity that his lips were wet...because of the wanton way she had shared that last wet, openmouthed kiss. "It's late," she said uncertainly. "You probably want me to go in—"

"I want you," he muttered, "right here."

His leather jacket cracked when he pulled her closer. His cupped hand buried in her hair, holding her, and then he dipped down to claim her mouth again. Her pulse skidded down a fast racetrack, even as warning bells clamored in her mind. Maybe she hadn't been around a city block, but any woman knew when she was in over her head. These weren't good-night smacks. These were headed for deep water, no paddle, no life jackets, and not a single buoy in sight.

"Rand—"

"Shh."

"Rand—"

"Shh."

Leigh felt his hand at her waist, tugging at the silk blouse that separated skin from skin. She could have stopped him. Her inhibitions were as fine-honed as instincts by now, and passion was no special lure. Whatever her limited experience, she'd had active hormones since fourteen. Anybody could subdue passion, and it was crazy to believe she was important to him.

But he made her feel that way. He made her feel as if she was earth and air and water, and he'd been deprived of them for a long time. His kisses burned, his touch was searching. He tasted warm and male. He tasted like naked desire and needs denied for much too long.

The stupid inn key was dangling into her palm. Leigh dropped it and reached for him. Her hand slid over his jacketed arm, up to his shoulder, then into the thick textured hair at his nape. When he'd kissed her at the castle, she'd felt the same fierce sense of rightness and belonging. It was crazy to feel it then. It was crazy now. She didn't care.

She heard the groan gather in his throat at her responsiveness, but there was nothing else she could do, no other choice. His embrace exposed a raw, dark loneliness, and he kissed that way. Like he was alone on the inside, like he'd found her, like nobody in the damn universe better take her away from him.

Good grief, she was right there. She pried her other arm free, framed his face. He took, kiss after kiss. She gave, kiss after kiss. His knee cracked against the dash and the windows fogged. He rubbed his beard against her cheek, an abrasive call to her senses, and then his lips tattooed a path down her throat, arousing a reckless summons of an entirely different kind.

Her spine arched, seeking closeness. The tips of her breasts crushed against his jacket, not him. Leigh wanted him. His palm had discovered bare skin under her blouse, and where he clutched and kneaded that soft flesh, she felt achy and hot. She wanted his hand to move up from her stomach. She wanted his lips to move down from her throat.

She wanted to make love with him, and she wanted it now, before the sweet, wild, reckless urgency disappeared. Thirty years old, and she'd never felt like this. This was how it was supposed to be, how she'd dreamed of feeling with the right man. Fever, like a hot scream inside her. Excitement, like a whispered rush of anticipation. And an overwhelmingly powerful tenderness, because the yearning and hunger in Rand were for her.

"Schöne," he whispered. *"Niedlich."* Frantic kisses slowly gentled. "Leigh." The sweeping, drugging caresses turned soothing. His dark eyes opened, as black as the devil's fire, and rested on her face.

He growled something else in German—not a word, Leigh expected, that was likely to be printed in her phrase book. He swore some more, gruffly, roughly, as he smoothed her blouse, feathered her hair back in place. "We're getting you out of this car. Quickly," he muttered darkly, but there was a hint of humor sneaking back into his eyes. "Dangerous thing, parked cars."

"I'm afraid I lost my key."

"I'm afraid I lost my head."

She took a breath. "I mean, I dropped the key when—"

"I know when. Exactly when." Another kiss, but this one was quick and hard, one of possessiveness and an apology at the same time. "I never meant to be rough. If I did anything to scare you, I'll poison myself," he offered.

Her lips started to curl. "That won't be necessary."

His head hunched over her knees. He swept the floor until he found her key, and when he leaned back up, his hair was boyishly disheveled, his jacket askew. "A parked *car,*" he grumbled again. "I had more finesse than this when I was sixteen, and ten times more control, and I had *no* control when I was sixteen. It's all your fault."

"*My* fault?"

"Well, it's sure not *my* fault that you're beautiful. And special. We're talking dangerous special, Ms. Merrick. What'd you do, pack buckshot in those kisses?"

"I never did," she assured him.

"Dynamite?"

"Not that, either."

"A secret drug, then? And please God, don't tell me it's a controlled substance."

By the time Rand escorted her to the door, she was laughing. His outlandish teasing took the awkwardness out of the moment, helped her pulse slow down to normal. It never occurred to her to take his exaggerated compliments seriously.

He turned the key in the lock, pushing open the door, and then lifted the key so she could see he was pocketing it in her purse. "Tomorrow, you won't have to worry about losing it. I'll confiscate any and all your keys when I pick you up at three."

"Rand—" Belatedly it occurred to her that this was how it all started—by her failing to take his invitation seriously. Then, she hadn't believed he wanted to go out with her again. Now, she was scared what would happen if they did.

"Wear old clothes." He was already striding for the car, becoming swallowed up in the foggy shadows. "We're going to be tromping around fields. I may be a few minutes late—I have a surgery scheduled right after lunch—but I shouldn't be much later than three."

"Rand—"

He stopped walking and turned to face the doorway where she stood. "Just say yes, Leigh. The last time you didn't say yes and I tried to persuade you, look how much trouble we got into. If I still have to convince you, we're going to wake Frau Stehrer, because I'm probably going to make a lot of noise chasing you up the stairs, and when I have you alone in your room—"

"*Yes.*"

"Yes?"

"Yes to tomorrow at three."

He grinned at her. "I *thought* that was what you were saying yes to. Pity." And then he was gone.

*   *   *

North two full blocks, Frau Stehrer had said. "You can't miss Franz's store, *fräulein*. The windows are full of clothes. Good strong clothes for hiking in the mountains. *North, fräulein*. You have figured out the north now, *ja?*"

Three blocks later, Leigh irritably spun around—no sign for *Franz* was anywhere in sight—and started backtracking.

A mongrel pup with floppy ears trailed at her heels. The pup had picked her up, as brazen as a hitchhiker, the moment she'd left the inn. Behind the pup, lagging by a few steps, was a freckle-faced urchin with suspenders holding up his short lederhosen.

It was no different than home, Leigh thought glumly. Stray dogs and bored kids always found her in Kansas, too.

For the second time that morning, she neared Herr Pfiefer's. And for the second time, she attempted to bolt, head down, past the baker's open door. It did no good.

"*Gruss gott,* Fräulein Merrick!"

Herr Pfeifer was rotund and round faced, with misleadingly kind eyes. Terribly misleading. Braced on his arm was a tray of confections that he was about to display in his front window. He lifted one, offering it to her.

"*Danke schön* so much; you are wonderfully kind, but no, honestly—"

"You will like. I promise. Fresh. Just this hour fresh, and *frei*. No cost. Just for you."

What was she supposed to do? Hurt his feelings? But Leigh insisted on paying—he had two sons in school—and she could hardly cut the conversation short because he liked to practice his English.

Walking along, five minutes later, she split the *pfannkuchen* with her two sidekicks. The powdered sugar melted on her tongue, as tempting as sin and hopelessly sweet. Herr Pfeifer had her accurately pegged as a sucker, she thought morosely. They all did. Only a week, and the whole town knew her weaknesses. The sophisticated makeup, the stylish, confident clothes, the hint of mystery in her smile . . . nobody was fooled.

Except for Rand.

There had been no chance of her sleeping the night before. He'd called her beautiful. He'd said it in velvet. He'd said she was dangerously special, and when his arms were around her, he had certainly made her feel that way.

She wasn't in his arms now. The morning was blindingly clear, the sun reflecting off the mountain peaks with a brilliant, painful glare. Last night she'd sensed that Rand was lonely, troubled about his grandfather, that he'd needed someone. Last night, she thought he'd needed *her*.

But she had woken up this morning feeling guilty and confused, and even a little scared. Maybe Rand had needed her, but Leigh was no longer sure who that *her* was—the woman who'd shocked herself with the force of passion she'd felt last night, or the plain old Leigh Merrick who probably couldn't find North if she were standing on the Pole.

"Franz," she muttered impatiently, and stepped off the curb to squint at all the shop signs up the next street. The boy politely delivered her a small lecture in

German. She didn't understand a word of it, but she had the nasty feeling that Wilhelm had already tried to tell her—several times—that she was headed in the wrong direction.

Eventually, feeling waves of relief, she found the store. Rand's directive had been to wear old clothes. Unfortunately, all her old clothes were in Kansas. She hadn't packed anything but new, fancy, faker's clothes—the stuff that was supposed to make her look poised and confident and daring. The stuff that was supposed to make her *feel* that way.

A bell tinkled when she opened the door. Both dog and boy tried to follow her inside. She dug into her left pocket for her last two spearmints and made motions that they could not come in.

The jig was up, she thought dryly. Tramping around the hills called for jeans. She looked like hell in jeans, hippy and dumpy, always had. You couldn't fool a man about your figure if you were wearing jeans.

She was almost glad. She no longer wanted to fool Rand about anything. She was a little scared, that too much, too easily, she had even started to fool herself.

They had company in the car—the peregrine, hooded and silent on his perch in the back seat. Leigh couldn't take her eyes off the bird.

Rand couldn't take his eyes off Leigh. When he picked her up, she had been as gregarious and warm as a best friend's sister. No one could be friendlier. No one could work so stubbornly hard to avoid direct eye contact.

She wanted to ignore last night with a capital *I*, Rand thought protectively. He suspected the only reason she'd shown up was to correct any dreadful misconceptions he'd formed the night before...like that she was a sensuous and passionate woman, exquisitely sensitive and unbelievably giving.

Rand hadn't formed any misconceptions.

The tires hummed as he took the mountain curves. He'd found a jewel. He didn't know how and he didn't know why, and the compelling reasons he had avoided serious relationships in the past still existed. Last night, he promised himself over and over that he would be more careful with Leigh, but he'd be damned if he wasn't going to enjoy being with her.

"What's his name, Rand?"

"Basta." He couldn't help a smile. The falcon clearly had her mesmerized.

"Are you sure it won't bother him that I'm here?" Her tone was a don't-wake-the-baby whisper.

"He's aware you're a new human scent, but as for worrying that he might be afraid of you—don't be. Basta isn't afraid of anything. It would never occur to him that anything so lowly and pitiful as a mere human being could conceivably trouble him."

She chuckled at Rand's description of Basta's massive ego. Only the seat belt inhibited her from completely leaning over the back seat, but she had stretched the strap as far as it would go. Her hair looked like gold washed in sunlight, and she'd worn a logen-green sweater tucked into jeans and hiking boots.

The logen-green sweater alluringly accented her full breasts, but Rand, personally, would have banished the garment to a closet. The fabric was wool, and far too likely to chafe her tender skin. Her jeans were

summer weight, tan rather than blue denim, and
brand-new. Not for the first time, he noticed that she
was slightly forgetful about tags. Rand knew the jeans
were new because the price tag was still stapled to her
right hip pocket. Contorted as she was to view the falcon in the back seat, he had a delectably clear view of
that curved right hip.

It was tough getting his mind off it. Sometime,
soon, he had to remove the tag before one of those
staples stabbed her. That could be tricky. Somehow he
had the feeling that Leigh might doubt his judiciously
solicitous motives if he put his hands on her fanny.

She'd be damn right, too.

"Tell me about them," she coaxed. "About the
birds. You train both falcons and hawks—what's the
difference? And how do you train them?"

The miles whizzed by as she kept up a steady bar-
rage of questions. Initially he was afraid of boring her,
but it was like pouring water through a sieve. The
more he answered, the more she wanted to know.

"Hawks and falcons are built differently—different tails, different length and shape of their wings—
but they're easiest to identify by temperament. A falcon's the aristocrat, a hawk the ruffian. Hawks are
high-strung, restless, nervous—they can be merciless
killers. Where a hawk can be mean, a falcon is mag-
nanimous. Proud. Intelligent. He's patient when he
hunts—patient and passionate."

"You wouldn't be slightly prejudiced toward your
falcons, would you?" Leigh teased.

"Maybe by a hair," he admitted.

"You train both the same way?"

He told her any bird of prey was trained the same way, and that the process was developed four thousand years by the Persians. "Nothing's changed since. The techniques are still the same. Basically the bird has to cross three milestones, each tougher than the last. First, he has to be 'manned'—meaning that he has to accept humans being around him. Some birds of prey never get past that. You're asking him, after all, to trust his most dangerous predator."

"And then?"

"Then, once he's developed the instinct to hunt, he has to get used to wearing the hood. He has to make the association that it's time to hunt, when and only when, that hood comes off. Again, that's an alien thing to his nature, but the third milestone—and the toughest one—is teaching the bird to 'lure.'"

"To lure?" Leigh echoed.

"To come back," Rand explained simply. "Once the hawk has caught his prey, he has no reason on earth to return to the falconer. Why should he? He's free, he's caught his meat, he isn't hungry. So the falconer has to coax him back with something, hopefully, that the bird wants more than his prey. I'll show you Basta's lure when we stop. It's a small leather cushion with different things tied to it—always fresh meat, but also bright feathers, dangling ribbons..."

"Basta likes ribbons?"

"Basta is a hopeless sucker for ribbons," Rand affirmed dryly.

"And that always works? It's as simple as having the right lure, and you can count on your bird to come home?"

He shook his head. "Lord, no. You can never count on the bird to return to you—it's never a sure thing. The falcon—or hawk—is completely free when he's in the air. He knows that. It has to be his choice to come home, based on the relationship he has with man."

Leigh fell silent while she thought about that. Rand could feel her eyes on his face. Whether she knew it, she'd kicked off a shoe and completely relaxed miles back. The sexual awareness between them was on a slow lazy simmer—there but easy, like the hum of a song one was coming to know. Talking reliably eased tension. Rand wanted her to feel natural and easy around him, but he was increasingly conscious that she avoided any mention of her own life.

She'd lost her parents young and had a witch in her background. That was all Leigh had told him—and then unwillingly. She had no reason to tell him anything, Rand reminded himself. Only she didn't strike him as a secret-hoarder or a fanatic about privacy. She was openhearted and giving with everyone around her. The only door she closed was on herself.

It bothered him. So much that he wondered what it would take to coax her to open that door.

Unfortunately he was afraid he already knew.

"Rand?"

He slowed down at they neared the place he wanted—a meandering stretch of clover-green meadow, strewn with wildflowers, open as far as the eye could see. No trees. A hawk could duck and dodge around trees, but the falcon's domain was mountain height and open sky. Basta, in the back, was becoming restive. He sensed where they were.

"Rand?" Leigh persisted. "From everything you told me, it's easy to understand how you became fascinated by your falcons. But everyone who's interested doesn't make a career from it. There had to be a personal draw for you—is it that you like to hunt?"

"I don't hunt," he immediately denied. "In fact, I've never killed anything in my life."

"You don't enjoy that part?"

"Not at all."

"I don't understand." Leigh shifted in her seat. "I thought that hunting was what the whole sport was about?"

Rand pulled over to the side of the road, thinking that there wasn't a woman on earth who'd ever gotten him to talk this much. Not about things that mattered. Not about things that were important to him.

"Hunting *is* what the sport is about—for the falcon. Basta hunts. That's what he was born for, what he lives for, what he loves." He hesitated. "I don't know why other falconers are involved. I just know why I am. You can tame a dog or a cat or a horse—but no one, ever in this life, will tame a bird of prey. His nature is wild and his spirit is free. Falconry is about getting a completely wild creature to willingly share something with you, trust you."

He leaned over and unsnapped Leigh's seat belt. His knuckles grazed her breast when he lifted the strap. The contact only lasted a second, yet she jerked like a scalded cat and her eyes flew to his. Sexual awareness sizzled between them like spit on a hot griddle. Poor baby, she'd worked so hard to put last night out of her mind. Rand hadn't. And couldn't.

"She's afraid of man," he continued calmly. "She should be. The only more successful predator on earth *is* man. So if she's going to come to him, honey, she has to believe that he won't hurt her. She has to believe that she's free to be her most natural, her wildest, her most vulnerable—the creature she was *meant* to be—with him."

Leigh sucked in a quick breath. "Rand?"

"Hmm?"

"You said 'she.' I thought you told me that Basta was a male."

A charming smile creased his cheeks—Leigh knew damn well he hadn't been talking solely about birds—and then he climbed out of the car. "Time's wasting, lady. About time you saw some action."

That, Leigh thought fleetingly, was what she was afraid of.

Five

Action. The next time Rand threatened to give her "action," Leigh thought two hours later, she was going to take him literally.

When she finally reached the car, her hair was straggling in her eyes; her thigh and calf muscles felt as if they'd just endured a hundred hours of straight aerobics; and a blister threatened her left front toe.

Rand was resettling a hooded Basta on the perch in the back seat. Neither of the boys, Leigh noted morosely, were even winded.

"Ready for a rest?" he asked her.

"Just a bit."

"There's a blanket in the trunk, if you want to spread it out. I brought some drinks in a cooler. Beer suit you okay?"

"Sounds great." Leigh didn't mention that she would have settled for dew licked off a leaf. Her throat was dryer than the desert in high summer. She found a blue plaid blanket in the trunk and wasted no time unfurling it on a stretch of grass. Not that she was whipped, but while Rand's back was still turned, she flopped down with more abandon than a tired puppy.

Late-afternoon sun, soporific and bright, shimmered down on her closed eyelids. Scents drifted in the wind—sharp clover, grasses, wildflowers, air so sweet it stung her lungs. When a shadow crossed her face, she never moved.

"Is it possible the lady isn't quite ready to take on Mount Everest at the moment?"

"Hey, I'm ready."

"I can see that," Rand said. "In the meantime, could the best sport I've met in a long time conceivably sit up long enough to satisfy her thirst?"

She opened one eye. The only thing on earth that could look better than the man hunched next to her was the tall stein of beer he held out. Perching up on one elbow, she gulped a few greedy swallows and then hesitated. No matter how thirsty she was, it had been several hours since lunch.

"I wouldn't worry about it. The local brews are called 'liquid bread.' They're not made like American beer. I'm not saying there isn't an alcoholic content, just that you can drink a lot more of this stuff before you ever feel an effect."

"Did you read my mind?" she asked him suspiciously. But because she believed him—and her throat was still hoarse-dry—she gulped down more sips of the tangy brew.

"When I asked the lady an hour ago if she wanted a drink," Rand mentioned casually, "she said she was fine. When I asked the lady—several times—if she was starting to wear down, she said, 'heavens, no'."

"I never said 'heavens, no' in that fakey soprano," Leigh denied.

"True. You said it in an unbearably sexy alto." Embarrassing the devil out of her, he hunkered down at her feet and tugged off her boots.

"Rand." She couldn't scold him about the boots. It felt too good to waggle her toes. "I wouldn't have missed a second of the last two hours for all the tea in China and England's crown jewels."

"Are you trying to tell me that you had a good time?"

"Good is a pale word, Krieger. I had the time of my life." By the time she drained the stein, Rand had unfolded beside her, one arm behind his head and his eyelids at half mast. Peeking through his beard was a satisfied grin. He looked life-of-Riley lazy, relaxed, and even marginally innocent.

Leigh wasn't fooled. She rolled on her stomach and propped her chin in a palm. It was a good position to study the most dangerous man she'd ever encountered. Although they were lying close as thieves, he made no move to touch her. That didn't make her feel any safer. In the sunlight his hair looked like dusty copper, all ruffled and disheveled; a boyish yank had fallen on his brow, and he must have been a little tired because all that vital virile energy was temporarily subdued. Those things didn't make her feel safer, either.

He'd scared her good this afternoon. Her pulse was still skipping; her heartbeat still thready, so much so that Leigh was tempted to laugh, at herself. By any rational criteria, nothing Rand had done could conceivably qualify for the labels of threatening or dangerous.

But she had never spent an afternoon in her life quite like this one.

It began simply enough. They'd hiked in the rough-rolling fields, at least a couple of miles if not more. The grasses were as tall as her knees, the sun warm on her shoulders. The falcon rode on Rand's arms. Leigh had kept waiting for something to happen, feeling like an awkward tagalong and worrying to death. She worried that she couldn't keep up. She worried that she'd embarrass Rand—or herself—if she did something wrong. She worried that she'd turn squeamish if the falcon actually killed something. Thankfully she didn't see anything the bird could hunt, but her senses weren't tuned to an awareness of wildlife.

Basta's were. Rand's were. One minute they were hiking, and the next Rand was whipping off the falcon's hook and untying the bird's leather jesses. He hurled Basta in the air, and the falcon seemed to fly straight for the sun.

Seconds passed, then minutes, before Leigh spotted a dozen grayish-brown birds, winging low from a knoll to the south. Basta was no more than a spot on the sun; they never noticed him. When the peregrine made its choice, he dived, suddenly, instantly, with the awesome speed of a streaking bullet.

Rand chose that moment to offer her a sip from the leather water pouch attached to his belt. He gently reminded her what he'd already told her about the difference between hawks and falcons. A hawk killed for the love of if—but that wasn't the falcon's nature. There was no malice in a peregrine; he hunted only when he was hungry, and his survival was dependent on that instinct.

Leigh had taken his water and understood precisely what Rand was trying to do with the little minilecture—divert her from the view of Basta overtaking his prey. His sensitivity to her feelings touched her, particularly when his concentration was captured elsewhere. His voice was hushed and his eyes never left the bird. His broad shoulders were braced in tension, alertness, anticipation, like part of his heart was in the sky.

Soon after, the falcon carried its limp prey to earth, dropped it, and hovered until Rand strode over and sacked the catch. To Leigh's horror, Basta took off again—completely disappearing from sight. She worried the falcon would never return, but it was as if the two, man and bird, communicated on their own private wavelength.

Long minutes passed with no sight of Basta, yet when Rand stretched out his arm, the peregrine was suddenly there, landing on his gloved wrist in a soft rush of flurried, regal feathers.

The bird was excited, euphoric, flustered...like a girl coming home from a prom date, like a boy who'd hit a home run. Rand fed him a treat, but it was obvious to Leigh that the tidbit wasn't the reward that Basta valued.

Rand whispered, crooned, talked. And talked. And talked—while jesses were retied and the hood resettled.

Rand's rapport with the falcon moved Leigh, shook her at an elemental level. They were not alike, yet the bond between them was intuitive. Rand never attempted to control or dominate the falcon's nature. It was exactly as he'd told her. The bird was free to be its most natural, its wildest, its most vulnerable—with him.

And that was when Leigh started to feel fear—although she'd be the first to admit it was a humorous, even silly fear. It was just so easy to imagine Rand unleashing that kind of intuitive power on a lover. Not Leigh, of course. Some other woman. But just to take herself, for the sake of an outlandishly far-flung example.

She had never felt natural with a man . . . yet Rand did something to make her forget her shyness. She didn't have a wild bone in her body . . . yet when he looked at her a certain way, when he touched her, she felt alive with longings wilder than a midnight wind. And she wasn't vulnerable. Good grief, a woman practical enough to wear rubbers in the rain could hardly label herself vulnerable. Only when she thought of Rand and rain, she didn't think of rubbers. Or umbrellas. She thought of kissing him, with the rain dripping off their eyelashes and their lips slick-wet, cool and hungry, thunder and they didn't give a damn, lightning and they didn't give a damn . . .

The fantasy died faster than a punctured balloon. When had the world gone so quiet? Rand was no longer catnapping, but leaning up on an elbow, wide-awake, studying her face with a watchful intensity.

Heat chased up her cheeks hotter than a scald, yet he did nothing, said nothing. It struck Leigh that she'd seen that same vigilant, protective expression before—when Basta had been flustered, Rand had responded by going completely quiet, completely still, as if willing the falcon to trust him.

It worked for the falcon. Not for her. If Rand guessed what she was thinking, she was going to bury her head in the nearest five feet of sand. "Heavens! Amazing how a little rest can revitalize a person!" she said cheerfully. "I feel like I could leap tall buildings in a single bound."

Superwoman fashion, give or take a lack of grace, she twisted around and attempted to lurch into a nice, proper, ladylike sitting position—only when her hip connected with the ground, she let out a surprised yelp. Something bit into her behind, as sharp as a tack.

Instinctively she rolled off the offended hip—and found herself jammed against Rand's chest. It wasn't her fault. Faster than she could blink an eye, he'd snaked an arm under her and hauled her over his chest. And quicker than she could clap a hand on her hurting posterior, Rand batted her hand away and dived his palm into her right hip pocket. He cupped her bottom with the familiar intimacy of a man who was well acquainted with women's bottoms. In fact, he...squeezed.

"Now just take it easy, Leigh," he instructed.

Take it easy? Her cheek was crushed against his sun-warmed throat, her breasts nuzzled against his ribs, her heart not likely to stop thumping in the near future. Still, she hadn't achieved a librarian's degree without some functioning brain power.

This just wasn't a kosher pickle. It had all the enticing look of a pass, but yanking a woman on top of him wasn't exactly Rand's style. The humor and patience lacing his voice lacked any claim to eroticism, and if he had sex on his mind, it was going to be tricky to pull off with his chin jammed on top of her head and a long muscled leg anchoring her still.

"This is not what you think."

Damn, she thought.

"The patch on your pocket was stapled in. One of them must have worked loose. My hand's between you and the staples so they can't poke you again, but just stay still, okay?" Once sure she understood, he lifted the weight of his leg off her. "I'll get that patch off."

"Rand?" She spoke directly to his chest.

"Hmm?"

"I think I'm going to die of embarrassment."

"Would it make it worse if I mentioned that you have an adorable, sexy fanny that I've been dying to get my hands on?"

"Much worse."

"I won't mention it then," he said gravely.

"Don't think I'm not grateful for your help," she said with equal gravity, "but I'm almost positive we could find an easier way to do this."

"We sure could. If you'd rather take off the jeans—"

"That isn't what I had in mind." There wasn't, truthfully, much on her mind except for the sensory overload from lying between his thighs. That wasn't necessarily his intention. When he'd grabbed her, she'd tumbled into the ignominious position. Only now his fly grazed her upper leg, and she couldn't move without rubbing against his zipper. She wasn't moving. Heck, she was trying her best not to breathe. What she'd classify as a delicate dilemma, though, seemed to ignite Rand's indefatigable sense of humor.

"Afraid you'll have to be patient. It'll probably take me another hour to get all four staples out—but not to worry. I'm being careful," he said virtuously. "I certainly wouldn't want to tear the fabric."

"Tear the fabric. Tear the fabric."

"Hey, do you think I'm enjoying this? Do you think I'm having fun?" he added in the husky tone of a conspirator. "Honey, you have the *warmest* tush—"

The instant his hand slid out of her pocket, Leigh scrambled free, but by then she was laughing. Rand *forced* her to laugh, the devil, by behaving so badly. He shook his hand and blew on it as if contact with her behind had threatened to burn him. She rained grass on his head and called him a ruthless tease. He produced the patch of proof of his innocence. She let him know what she thought of his "innocence."

And then he grabbed her hand.

The sunlight softened, the breeze stilled. If Rand's outrageous teasing had kindled her physical awareness of him, there'd been no risk, no harm. She knew him now. It wasn't the first time his play had been deliberate. It wasn't the first time he'd used shameless flirting to ease an awkward situation for her.

But he suddenly turned serious. His fingers steepled against hers, matching rough skin to soft, a calloused palm to her tender one. The laughter in his eyes

had been exchanged for a blue-diamond brightness.
"Leigh." His thumb tip rubbed softly, erotically, on
the pulse of her wrist. "You're special."

She shook her head.

"Yes, you are. More special than I know how to tell
you. You make the world seem lighter when I'm
around you. Lighter, brighter, a gentler place."

She shook her head again, this time more fiercely.

He responded by leaning closer, too close, with a
narrowed, considering look in his eyes. She had the
feeling that denying his compliment was a mistake.
She had the feeling he was wrestling with something—a decision, a choice. She had the feeling that
while he was suddenly thinking so hard, right now, she
could sneakily edge a nice, healthy distance away from
him.

Wrong. His hand caught her wrist like the slow, lazy
curl of a lariat. His hold was gentle. She just wasn't
going anywhere.

"You cut yourself down, honey. There's no reason. You can't possibly not realize how unique you
are," he said quietly. "For one thing—nothing throws
you. Meeting my grandfather when he's in one of his
moods would knock most people for six. Not you.
Drag you over ten miles of hills and dales. You're up
for it. Even when a man came apart on you in the
front seat of a car, because you were just so damn
open and giving that he lost his head—"

"Rand . . ." Jeez-louise, she had to stop this. He
didn't know the real Leigh at all. Everything on earth
threw her. She had inhibitions for every occasion and
extras for holidays, and it was past time she owned up.
"I'm not who you think I am."

All she said was the simple truth. It was hardly the equivalent of waving a red flag in front of a bull. Yet Rand's eyes suddenly darkened with resolve, and he released her wrist—but only to free his own hand. Fingertips framed her face, sieved through her hair, his touch as heady as a secret and as hypnotic as his warm breath. "What I think is that you're a beautiful, sensual woman..."

Too much sun, she thought desperately. He must have had too much sun.

"...with a rare brand of courage. Not every woman has the guts to travel halfway across the world alone."

Oh, God. A thirtieth birthday and a case of despair had motivated her packing, nothing remotely related to guts. "You have it all wrong—"

"I don't think so." His thumb feathered across her bottom lip. "I think you have more courage than you know what to do with, honey. Most people find a lone wolf, they run like hell. You'd take him home. You'd listen to him. You'd offer him compassion and empathy, and you'd make him laugh, and you'd remind him of all the things he'd been missing."

"Rand—"

"Yeah. I'm not talking about wolves. I'm talking about men, and I'll bet you've given a lot of men grief, Merrick. Because I can't imagine a man who wouldn't find you dangerously exciting—"

Leigh couldn't listen anymore. She just couldn't. Rand was so completely wrong about her that she was going crazy.

So she wrapped her arms around him and tugged him down, where she could hold him tight. She held him tight because it was all she knew how to do. And she kissed him wantonly, brazenly, openly . . . because tarnation, he was under the insane impression she was like that, anyway.

Her strategy was brilliantly effective. Rand never said another word.

He also never pushed nor threatened to deepen the embrace. He was just there, like the glow of a banked fire on a cold night, offering acceptance and warmth and the shelter of his strong arms. It was her own doing, her own fault that she was suddenly aware of the mesh of their heartbeats, the pulsing rush shooting low to her stomach, her rocketing response to his taste, his scent, his weight. Only at the precise moment she realized she was wallowing in waters way over her head, Rand lifted his head and smiled at her.

A soft smile. A tender man's smile. A reward, that smile, for nothing more than being a woman. And then his lips dropped down and delivered a kiss, a cherishing, treasuring kiss—nothing fast and awkward and desperate, like hers. His kiss was agonizingly slow and complete. His kiss was designed to make a woman believe she was the sun and the moon and precious beyond price.

Leigh wasn't precious. She was no man's treasure. She'd have told him.

She tried. Her blue-eyed falconer had certainly wanted to talk before. Now, he'd definitely changed his mind.

"Where is she?" Rand asked Frau Stehrer in German.

"I'm supposed to guess who 'she' is, with all the women you know, Rand Krieger?" Greta automatically filled a mug of strong, hot coffee and pushed it across her kitchen counter. "Sit down for a minute and dry off. I can't understand it. Yesterday, the weather was so nice and half my boarders stayed inside. This morning, the whole world seems determined to be out in this incredible downpour."

"Did—" But he had no chance to finish the question.

"How is your grandfather?"

"Good today—"

"And Jannette? She is working out for you all right?"

The good frau was referring to the fourth housekeeper she'd sent to the Krieger house. Theodor had a way of scaring off hired help almost faster than Rand could hire them. "She's working out fine, even talking about moving in during the weekdays, and I thank you—again—for sending her to us. But in the meantime—"

Finally Greta, who could be as hard to escape as a spider web, took pity on him. "*Ja, ja, ja. She* went out about an hour ago, she said to buy some postcards. To the pharmacy."

"*Danke.*" Rand took a fast gulp of coffee, rapped his knuckles on the counter, and strode for the door.

"Wait."

He turned around in the doorway.

"I told you she was headed for the pharmacy," Greta reminded him.

"And I heard you."

"The pharmacy is west of here two blocks."

"Frau Stehrer, I've been living here for seven years. Obviously I know where the pharmacy—" He checked

himself, and for the first time all morning, chuckled.
"You told her west?"

"Clearly."

"And she's been gone how long?"

"An hour now. And thankfully on foot." Greta
made a reverent sign of the cross. "Because of the
storm, she was considering taking the car she rented.
You have seen her drive? An experience guaranteed to
renew your faith in God." She advised, "Keep her off
the streets."

"I intend to," Rand assured her, and promptly
headed east.

Twenty minutes later, though, he still hadn't tracked
Leigh down. She couldn't be out in the pouring rain—
no one was. He poked his head in several shops. In the
height of the ski season no one could keep track of
individual tourists. But this was spring, and as Rand
could have guessed, there wasn't a shop owner or
townsperson who didn't know Leigh. A few had seen
her—enough so he knew he was headed in the right
direction—but that was only so much help.

The morning was as dark as pitch, the rain unre-
lenting. An occasional car streaked by, spattering water, and walking was an exercise in dodging puddles.
Rain matted in his eyelashes, soaked in his hair, riveled down the back of his neck. He wore a parka, but
it was ineffective protection against this kind of rain.
He could have driven, but a car was no way to find a
woman on foot.

Especially a woman on foot who might not want to
be found.

He stopped at a street corner, studying the shop
signs, trying to outguess where she might go. *Likely*

NO COST! NO OBLIGATION TO BUY! NO PURCHASE NECESSARY!

PLAY "LUCKY 7" AND GET AS MANY AS SIX FREE GIFTS...

HOW TO PLAY:

1. With a coin, carefully scratch off the silver box at the right. This makes you eligible to receive one or more free books, and possibly other gifts, depending on what is revealed beneath the scratch-off area.

2. You'll receive brand-new Silhouette Desire® novels. When you return this card, we'll send you the books and gifts you qualify for *absolutely free!*

3. If we don't hear from you, every month we'll send you 6 additional novels to read and enjoy. You can return them and owe nothing but if you decide to keep them, you'll pay only $2.47* per book, a saving of 28¢ each off the cover price. There is *no* extra charge for postage and handling. There are *no* hidden extras.

4. When you join the Silhouette Reader Service™, you'll get our subscribers'-only newsletter, as well as additional free gifts from time to time, just for being a subscriber.

5. You must be completely satisfied. You may cancel at any time simply by sending us a note or a shipping statement marked "cancel" or by returning any shipment to us at our cost.

*Terms and prices subject to change without notice.
Sales tax applicable in N.Y.
© 1990 HARLEQUIN ENTERPRISES LIMITED

This lovely Victorian pewter-finish miniature is perfect for displaying a treasured photograph— and it's yours absolutely free—when you accept our no-risk offer.

SILHOUETTE "NO RISK" GUARANTEE
- You're not required to buy a single book—ever!
- You must be completely satisfied or you may cancel at any time simply by sending us a note or a shipping statement marked "cancel" or by returning any shipment to us at our cost. Either way, you will receive no more books; you'll have no obligation to buy.
- The free books and gifts you receive from this "Lucky 7" offer remain yours to keep no matter what you decide.

If offer card is missing, write to:
Silhouette Reader Service, 3010 Walden Ave., P.O. Box 1867, Buffalo, N.Y. 14269-1867

*any possible place she'd think you wouldn't look,
Krieger.*

He plodded on, mentally damning himself from
here to hell for failing to do what he should have done
yesterday afternoon. Handcuff her neatly to his side.

Instead, he'd taken her back to the inn. The thing
was, he had Basta to get home, his grandfather to take
care of, an evening meeting he couldn't cancel. Leigh
understood—he'd told her ahead that he only had the
afternoon free—and it made no sense to drag her
through a night of chores and responsibilities that
couldn't possibly interest her. So he'd believed then.

Now he believed differently.

He should have dragged her.

He pushed the dripping hair from his brow. Images
raced through his mind. Images that had sharpened
and magnified through a sleepless night. Her hair
spread out on the blanket, strands of taffy and dark
honey and pure gold. Lips, lush and red-wet. Her
breasts, bared for the sun, full and swollen and taut.
The sounds she'd made when he'd slid the zipper down
her jeans....

The look in her eyes when he'd rolled away from
her.

He hadn't played with matches that hot since he was
a kid. Nothing should have gone that far. At first he'd
only intended to bolster her confidence. Once too often, Leigh had shied away from a compliment. Once
too often, she'd denied anything nice said about her.
The damn blonde. She *was* special. She *was* passionate and sensitive; she reached out with warmth and
caring; she made a man feel too damn good for *her*
own good. So he'd told her.

Only hell.

Rand had no idea she'd react by throwing her arms around him. What bothered his conscience was that he should have. He'd discovered before that daring her, teasing her, was a definite key to coaxing Leigh into opening up.

What she did was understandable. What he did was inexcusable. Rand never lost control in a sexual situation—he wouldn't do that to a woman, any woman, and especially not to an innocent like Leigh. He didn't care how many men she had or hadn't known. She was new at love. So new that her body's responses startled her...so new that she was unaware of tempting a loaded gun...so new that it was a joy to watch her testing her wares, risking her wiles, slowly gaining confidence that no roof would fall on her feminine head if she dared touch him, dared enjoy being touched.

He'd coaxed the confidence out of Leigh, all right.

And had his shaken good. Seconds later and he'd have made love to her—and what killed him most—not regretted it.

But Leigh would have. And when she hadn't answered the phone this morning, he knew—sensed-in-his-gut *knew*—that he'd scared her.

Rand passed the perfumerie, the green grocer, the antique shop and jeweler's. No Leigh. Lightning crowned the jagged mountaintops; thunder roared through the valley; water riveled down the cobblestone streets. He'd reached the edge of town. Still no Leigh, and he was running out of places to look.

Not that he was discouraged.

He'd find her.

Six

———

Leigh had been twelve years old when she discovered the ideal sanctuary, the perfect hideout, the one place where no one could possibly guess where she was.

When the thunderstorm turned wild and windy, she was forced to seek shelter. The moment she walked into the Hautberg library, though, she knew her choice of refuge was no accident.

As she tugged off her scarf and drenched raincoat, her senses inhaled the familiar smells of books and dust and leather bindings. Where her Kansas library was relatively new, this one was an old converted house with books sectioned off in a dozen tiny rooms. Maybe the trappings were different, but the place was the same. Off the lobby, she saw a red-haired woman—obviously the librarian—talking to a bean-stalk-thin gentleman near the card catalog. Wet coats hung on chair backs—typical of a rainy weekday morning. Books were piled on a rolling cart, waiting to be checked in. Leigh knew the whole routine.

No one noticed her walk in. She looked no different than the other soggy storm refugees—squeaking wet shoes, dripping bangs—but her appearance wouldn't have mattered regardless. Not here. Leigh always thought it a miracle that criminals had never discovered the intrinsic anonymity of libraries—no one looked at you, so how could there be a better place to hide?

She felt just a tad like a criminal herself as she slipped up the narrow staircase to the second floor. Rand had promised to call this morning. Maybe he had. Maybe he hadn't. Either way, she had no reason to think he was looking for her. She just felt better knowing that no one—not even a hawk-eyed falconer—was going to find her here.

Upstairs she found what she was looking for—the children's room—and for a few minutes simply wandered around. Outside it was as dark as a tomb and rain battered the windows, but here the curtains were a cheerful red, the walls decorated with paper balloons, and bright-jacketed books displayed to tempt the little ones. Three urchins were sprawled on a round braided rug, fingering picture books, alone, left no doubt by a mother who didn't want to drag her kids shopping in the rain. Leigh knew that routine, too.

She didn't start working by intent. Keeping half an eye on the children—the librarian downstairs was obviously busy—it just happened that she found a book out of place. And then another and another. There wasn't a single tome in English, but the Dewey decimal system was universal. Leigh considered it a credit to the librarian that the shelves were an absolute mess. Untouched books were unused books. This children's reference section was getting a wonderful workout.

She was interrupted once—the blonde in pigtails chose to hit her younger sibling, a problem solved easily enough with her sternest librarian's scowl and a handful of gum drops—but after that, she lost track of time.

By the time she'd worked up to 598.29, the sleeves of her gold sweater were pushed up and her white corduroy skirt had a dust smudge. She was kneeling on the dusty wooden floor, four stacks in, scouting the decimal numbers on the bottom shelf of books. Should the librarian pop in, Leigh figured she risked getting hauled off to the Hautberg equivalent of a funny farm, but she didn't care. The work felt good. For the first time since she'd set foot on Austrian soil, she was doing something natural to her. She knew books. She understood books.

She did *not* understand what happened yesterday.

Making love with brazen abandon in an open meadow—it wasn't Leigh. She still had whisker burns on her cheeks. More embarrassingly, she still had whisker burns on her breasts. What that man could do with his beard redefined wicked. What he could do with his hands defied description. And Leigh was mortifyingly aware that long before Rand stopped, she would have done anything he asked, any way he asked.

At one o'clock in the morning... and two... and three... she had been pacing her bedroom floor, mentally laying an Aunt Matilda-styled guilt trip on herself. Lust wasn't love. She had a galloping set of deprived hormones, which Rand couldn't know. She'd be crazy to misinterpret her own feelings as love, and unfortunately, there was no way to misinterpret Rand's.

Thanks to her stupid, shallow game of pretending to be someone else, he thought she was brave. He thought she'd had lots of men in her life. He'd called her passionate and—criminatly—dangerously exciting.

He couldn't love her.

He didn't even *know* her.

All he knew was the faker. Leigh shoved a book back into place without even looking at it, and rocked back on her heels. With a dusty hand, she swiped at her tired eyes. All the heavy-duty guilt and self-condemnation had kept her up last night. Unfortunately, they hadn't done any good.

What she remembered happening in the meadow…it wasn't as simple as lust. Rand had made her feel cherished and desired and needed. He'd homed to her arms with dark, lost eyes and precious rough-tender kisses. "I swear I won't let this go too far, Leigh," he'd promised her with a tone so harsh it made her heart ache, and he was wrong. For her, it had gone too far the minute she realized that his hands were unsteady, that she wasn't getting experienced kisses and clever skilled embraces but raw emotion. How damn long had he been alone? *That* alone?

Leigh had responded because she cared. And even when the fire and smoke cleared, she felt the same way. Staying up all night hadn't changed her feelings. Filing all these books wasn't helping, either. Nothing, in her entire life, had felt so natural or right as being with him.

So what are you going to do, Merrick?

A silly question. If she had any idea what to do, she'd hardly be hiding out in the Hautberg public library, scared of more things than she could count. Scared she meant nothing to him. Scared she did. Scared she'd feel that incredible, impossible, *stupid* sense of rightness when she saw him again. Scared she wouldn't. Scared he'd find out she was a faker, a nobody, a thirty-year-old dying-on-the-vine spinster from Kansas. Scared...

"Hi."

Scared she was becoming delusional, because it sounded like Rand's voice—when it obviously couldn't be. Not only was the library a guaranteed sanctuary, but being in the children's room doubled her protection. A ship lost in the Devil's Triangle had an equal chance of being found.

"Leigh?"

A pair of long lean legs hunkered down beside her. She saw his boots were dripping; his open parka was dripping and he smelled like rain and wet wool.

She looked up. Crystal droplets clung to his beard, his hair was damp at the temples, and his eyes had to be as dark and blue as ink in water. Thunder shuddered just outside. She didn't hear. The lights flickered. She didn't notice.

He'd been looking for her—the lines of pure bulldog tenaciousness were still etched on his face. She only had a glimpse of that steel, only had seconds to catch the dreadful clue to his character. Hiding from the rest of the world was easy. Hiding from Rand was a futile exercise. He didn't, wouldn't give up. And he didn't—at all—like losing things that mattered to him.

His sober gaze roamed her face, searching, studying, and then he smiled. Had she given away how much she wanted to see him? He reached up and brushed a tendril of hair from her cheek, the gesture soothing more than sexual, yet protective. Intimately protective. He'd had the same look in his eyes when he'd stopped their lovemaking in the meadow yesterday.

"When I was a kid," he mentioned, "I used to spend rainy days in a library. You, too?"

"Me, too."

He nodded. "Books are supposed to keep a kid out of trouble. Not me. About eight years old, I got into books about falcons, and that started an addiction I've never been able to shake. I blame it all on rainy days and libraries." As though he'd come here for no other purpose, he hefted a book from the stack near her knees, glanced at the spine and then shelved it. "Come on, confess. With you, the hook was fairy tales, wasn't it?"

"When I was a kid."

"Yeah, I'll bet you liked all those princes and knights. I just couldn't see it, all those guys running around in tights. Except for my dad—who's the best man I knew—I kind of leaned toward heroes of the wild West variety."

She watched him shelve another book. In the wrong place. She didn't stop him. "Wild West?"

"You're probably too young to remember Wyatt Earp and Bat Masterson and Cheyenne and Wild Bill Hickock. Hell, I only caught them on the reruns, but

I'll tell you—they were some heroes. Seems like kids today get the short end of that stick. Watch TV, and you'd get the impression the only good guys around are burned-out cops." He finished shelving the books. "Maybe it's a good thing there are still rainy days and libraries. Honey, I shouldn't have left you yesterday afternoon."

He slipped in the last comment like a fastball from left field. Leigh hadn't known when it was coming, only that something had to. Rand was still dripping rain, still hunkering down in his parka, and he hadn't tracked her to the children's section of the Hautberg library to have an innocuous conversation about conceptual heroes. Or maybe, indirectly, he had. Until that moment, it hadn't occurred to Leigh that he'd worried about failing her or hurting her.

"You didn't 'leave me,' Rand. The afternoon was all you had free. You'd already told me you had responsibilities last night. There was no problem."

"Nothing we can't solve, anyway." He pushed to his feet and extended a hand. "Any chance you know where your shoes are?"

"Shoes?" Grave as a judge, he motioned to where her stockinged toes peeked out from under her skirt edge. Valiantly she struggled for dignity. "I don't usually take off my shoes in a public place. It was just they were so wet when I came in—"

"It's a wet, nasty day," he agreed. "But it's getting better. Or it will—once we've found a fire, something to eat and a big mug of something hot to drink. Assuming, of course..." There was a devilish twinkle in his eyes "...that we can find your shoes."

Lunch alone with him struck her as a terrible idea. "Rand, I just don't think—" He grasped her hands and pulled her to her feet. "I mean, you probably have things you need to do. And I've already taken up a lot of your time. And I'm not at all hungry. And—"

Rand released her hands, only to loop his arms around her neck. She felt short without shoes. At least next to him, and he had to bend to nuzzle his brow against hers. That was all he did—and then only for seconds—but it was enough to remind her of all the terrible things that happened when they were this close. Her lungs intook air in chunks. Her heart accelerated faster than a jet taking off. On the inside, she felt softer than velvet, valued and cherished, and the witless rattle she had for a mind started spinning fantasies about what the two of them could be together.

"Leigh." Rand lifted his head. Something had happened to his voice—probably a chill from the rain—that put an erotic huskiness in his tone. "For the record I would have torn up this town if I had to, honey. I need to talk with you. You're not really going to give me an argument, are you?"

She closed her eyes. "No." Her mind wasn't half as clouded as she wished it were. Her compelling physical reaction to Rand only underlined how deeply she had come to care about him. It had gone too far. It was long past time to be completely honest with him. "I need to talk with you, too."

Leigh wasn't nervous. If anything, she felt relieved as Rand led her to a private booth at the back of a quiet bar a few minutes later. Deceit had preyed on her conscience long enough. She was determined that it was all coming down . . . the life-style of a wallflower, the kids, the cats, the crunch of a thirtieth birthday and her idiotic game. Courage wasn't even in her vocabulary. She intended to be sure Rand knew. Her major experiences with passion had come vicariously from novels. She was even going to confess that.

As Leigh shucked her raincoat and slid into the secluded booth, she glanced around. The nearly empty tavern had an ideal atmosphere for a private conversation. The decor was Robin Hood medievalish—forest greens and stained glass and candles in pewter holders. A huge soot-stained fireplace took up one wall, big enough to roast a boar and toast the entire place in winter. Now, only a small fire crackled in the open grate, scenting the room with fragrant, soothing wood smoke.

It was nice and dark, she thought. Dark enough to make an awkward conversation easier, yet not so gloomy she couldn't clearly see Rand across the table.

The opposite, of course, was also true. This close, with a yellow candlestick flickering between them, there was nothing she could hide from Rand. When she reached for a menu, a flop of hair drooped over her right eye. She pushed it away. It flopped back again. Thanks to a double drenching in rain, her hairstyle no longer existed and her makeup foundation was long gone. Likely every freckle was exposed. She knew she'd chewed off her lipstick.

It was tempting to race for the rest room to repair the damages, but Leigh refrained. This showdown was about honesty. She wanted Rand to see who she was— who she *really* was. Beneath the booth, she slipped off her damp shoes and curled a leg under her, mentally gearing up for her little talk about why he *really* couldn't want to be involved with her.

"Honey?"

An hour later, she could pin down the precise moment her great intentions went to the dogs. It started with the gentle, possessive way Rand said that "honey," and deteriorated when he asked what she wanted for lunch.

Abruptly Leigh discovered there was a limit to her appreciation of authentic medieval lore. The menu entrées included venison, wild boar and suckling pig. Her expression made Rand chuckle. He suggested that she order the native Waller. The fish was delectable, so was the *spätzle* and apple wine, but to inject her agenda into the conversation—there was just no way.

In a teasing, relaxed mood, Rand was hard to resist, but he definitely controlled the conversation. Until the plates were cleared and the coffee served, Leigh didn't realize that his banter was deliberate and that something was wrong. Not with her. With him.

"You can't, honey, come to Austria without seeing Vienna. Or the Lake District. And music—you need to hear an opera while you're dressed to the gills. And you need to experience gypsy music by an open fire in a field at night."

Rand's tone was seductive, coaxing—but the rogue's patter didn't match the driven intensity in his gaze. Still, there was no specific reason why she was worried about him. The conversation couldn't be more low key. Rand would have her believe the only thing on his mind was listing every tourist attraction in Austria.

"...and castles. I know how you feel about castles. It took a little studying, but I finally found the one that will make up to you for missing your Sleeping Beauty Neuschwantstein. The name is Waterschloss Anif—it's owned by a count, located just south of Salzburg, easily done in a day trip, and it even has a fairy tale attached to it."

"You don't have to make up to me for missing anything—"

"Aren't you going to ask me which fairy tale?"

Leigh cupped her chin in her palm, and figured she might as well sucker in. "Which one?"

"Cinderella. You know. The one with the shoe." His eyes flashed with humor. "Right?"

"Well up on your fairy-tale plots, are you?"

"Well enough to know the catalyst for Cinderella is a shoe and the catalyst for Sleeping Beauty is a kiss. Speaking from a man's viewpoint, I favor the plot with some definite body contact—"

Leigh decided she was going to come back in the next life and spank him. He reached over, as innocent as a boy, and lifted the silky strand drooping over her right eye.

"But the point is not the fairy tale. It's all those places that you need to see—none of which you can see alone. That's the law in Austria."

"The law," she echoed. "I had no idea."

"What can I say?" He shrugged helplessly. "You're not in America now. In Austria we have a lot of different laws, unbreakable laws, laws set in stone—"

"In Austria, you seem to have an extraordinary number of fast-talking flirts."

"That, too," he readily concurred. "In fact, that's another reason why you can't go touring the countryside alone. You have no idea how dangerous Austrian men are—how could you? The boys in this part of the country were raised from the cradle to be subtle with a woman, to shower her with compliments and disarm her guard and then wham!" He snapped his fingers. "The big bad wolf moves in."

"Maybe the lady is old enough to handle a big bad wolf."

"American wolves, yes. But Austrian wolves, no way, Jose."

"Maybe the lady is a little wary of this highly generous offer to protect her." She didn't mean a loaded innuendo. She was just trying to flirt back with him in kind, yet there was a sudden change in atmosphere, like the storm's electric charge had moved inside. She found herself bracing without knowing why.

"Some people might warn you that you should be wary," Rand agreed, and hunched forward. He didn't touch her, but his eyes pulled her in, wrapped her in, captured her attention with the same power as a physical caress. "Leigh, listen to me."

"I am."

"I've been around. My share, maybe more than my share," he said quietly. "That can look wrong to a woman. Most men my age are past the hunt and chase and have settled down—unless they were shallow turkeys incapable of commitment to begin with. I know how it looks, but I'm telling you, honestly, that's not how it is."

"Rand, I never said I thought—"

"I have roots in two countries, but a home in neither. I'm caught in between. There's no way in hell I'm giving up my own country, and no way in hell I can— or would—leave my grandfather. And what that amounts to is that I had to put my personal life on hold. I wouldn't involve a woman in my life, Leigh. Not until those circumstances change, and I have some security and stability to offer. You hear me?"

She heard him. More, she watched herself suddenly sinking in emotional quicksand. Rand flirted as easily as some men brushed their teeth, but laying out his feelings—he hadn't before. He didn't like to. He didn't want to.

The talk about honesty she'd planned to have with him wasn't going to happen. She knew it, knew it was unconscionable to postpone it again, yet she was stuck. Rand was simply the greater priority.

It was possible—not wise, not sensible, not practical, not sane—but possible she was falling in love with Rand. Not because of his baby blues and his honor and his sensitivity and control and devil's own dry humor, but because he was so damned *wrong*.

The falconer seemed to think his grandfather was a complication to a relationship. He was right. He seemed to think that some women might be wary of picking up stakes for an indefinite number of years in a foreign country. He was right. And so dead wrong that she could shake him. Those were only hurdles to cross, not mountains, not for a woman who loved him. People who loved each other worked things out.

"What I'm trying to tell you, honey, is that you're safe with me. I'm not looking for something serious. And you're only going to be here a few weeks, so

there's no way you could want something complicated. What that adds up to, if you think about it, is
that we're playing by the same stakes."

"Rand—"

But he wasn't going to give her a chance to respond. "I want to spend time with you. I want to show
you my Austria, to be with you, laugh with you, enjoy what happens whenever we seem to be together.
And I think you want the same thing."

She was just slipping her hand under the table when
he caught it. He made a tent of their hands, a bridge,
and then his fingers laced between hers and held. He
said softly, bluntly, "What happened yesterday is in
your eyes every time you look at me. So you got
shook, Leigh, and maybe because we edged darn close
to an abyss—but I'll be damned if you don't trust me.
I stopped us. You know that. There's no way I can
promise not to touch you, but I can promise you I
won't lose control. The last thing I want is to hurt you,
honey. Would you believe that?"

The bartender started toward them with the check.
Leigh waved him off. Moments before the waitress had
hovered with a fresh coffeepot. Leigh had waved her
off, too. Rand seemed to have forgotten they were in
a public tavern.

Leigh knew exactly where they were, knew that it
should have been her nature to flush and fluster the
moment intimacy entered the conversation. Somehow she wasn't flustering. Later, she would remember his promise of control as a gentleman's honor put
on the line. They weren't going to make love. Not if
Rand had anything to say about it.

At that precise moment, though, her center of gravity was not the specific conversation but simply the man sitting across from her. Rand was communicating loneliness. He was communicating need, and from the inside out, her most feminine instinct was to respond with what she felt—caring and love.

"Leigh—"

"I believe you. I'm also glad you cleared the air. I can't think of a better way for us to both be sure we want the same things." It rang a little false, but Leigh buried that qualm of conscience. It wasn't Rand's problem that she was over-her-head involved. She simply had to make sure he never knew, and she smiled for him—a smile with all the gutsy confidence of a woman who really thought she knew what she was doing. "Come on, Krieger. Let's blow this pop stand. You and I have things to do and see."

Seven

The low stone building that housed the falcons smelled of straw and feathers and something indefinably wild. It was no place to walk in evening clothes and heels, but Leigh didn't mind.

Hawks were kept separate from falcons, birds in training isolated from fledgling young ones, and one section—Leigh privately called it the Honeymoon Hotel—was devoted to breeding pairs. She counted the cream-and-brown eggs in the peregrines' nesting boxes, whispered greetings to the birds she knew, and paused to admire a huge black-and-white gyrfalcon—Julia, a new edition.

Rand was under the mistaken impression that she was safely stashed in his hospital office, out of harm's way. Their quick getaway, not for the first time this week, had been interrupted by the arrival of an injured bird. "I won't be long," he'd promised her.

She'd heard that one before. The gentle lecture that followed was also familiar. "Birds of prey are not like cats and dogs, honey. They're wild and unpredictable. It's just safer not to wander around unless I'm with you."

Leigh had dutifully waited until he was out of sight before stealing out to the falcons—not for the first time. Rand didn't need to know, she reasoned. Since he'd shown her the birds himself, she knew his attitude was overprotective. All the birds were caged. They couldn't hurt her, never tried, and being alone with them gave Leigh the chance to enjoy and learn. She enjoyed the birds. She learned—about Rand.

Her mood was inevitably thoughtful as she ducked outside through a low arched door. Judging from the inside of the house, Rand could pack for home at a moment's notice. Except for his grandfather, he had no ties in Austria. So he'd told her. So he believed.

Pity he was too big to give a good shaking, Leigh mused. The truth just wasn't as simple as he wanted it to be. His heart was in those falcons, and maybe he had tried to remain unattached, but short-term goals hadn't held him long. The whole setup was extensive and complex, his breeding program ambitious and long-term.

In the west, the sun had just dipped behind a mountain. A blush of pink stained the whole sky. Plum trees blossomed on the grassy ridge, scenting the evening with their sweetness, and the lawn stretched down to the woods like a lush spread of green cashmere. Leigh didn't, couldn't linger. Over the past

week, she'd discovered that a mountain sunset over
Krieger land was an addictive danger. She was prey to
a heady sense of belonging, to the mountains, to the
life here, to the man.

Years ago, thankfully, she'd learned what to do with
impossible dreams—drown them in an ocean of re-
pression. That was easy. How to help Rand was a
tougher problem. Whether he knew it or not, he
wasn't leaving here. All week, she'd been waiting for
a chance to tackle him about it . . . which occasionally
struck her sense of humor.

The old Leigh, in her most flagrant fantasies, would
never have tackled a man about anything.

The new Leigh was faking brazen guts fairly well—
caring about Rand was miraculously its own momen-
tum—but once in a while she reverted to type. Like
now.

One glance at her watch, and she flew across the
gravel path toward the small hospital building. As
quiet as a cat, she pulled open the door. Like the keep
that had housed falcons for centuries, the converted
minivet hospital was built of solid stone. Inside were
cool, whitewashed walls, tiled floors and a familiar
antiseptic smell that made her nose crinkle. Her heels
made such a guilty clatter that she tiptoed in. Rand's
operating room was located at the turn of a corner.
His office—where she was supposed to be for the last
half hour—was two doors closer.

"It's too late, *fräulein*. I already saw you sneaking
out, and I know exactly what you've been up to."

She spun around, her hand at her throat. The man
striding toward her would have startled anyone. His
tone was severe, his bearing military correct, his height

daunting, and beneath a mane of white hair was a forbiddingly condemning scowl. Leigh pursed her lips. "Are you gonna tell on me?"

"As if I would. A Krieger would never tell tales on a beautiful woman. I have told you and told you."

"I'm sorry. I forgot." With a warm smile, she severed the few steps between them. Rand's grandfather never invited the peck on his cheek, but ever gallant, he discreetly stooped down so she could deliver it.

"Did you enjoy the birds?" With an old rogue's twinkle, he straightened, and calmly plucked a twig of straw from her hair. "Never mind. I can see you did. Turn around, Leigh, so I can assess for further damages before my grandson finds you. Where are you headed tonight?"

Obligingly she turned around to face the blank whitewashed wall. "I'm not sure of the location. Rand said there was some kind of festival. Gypsy music." She'd dressed in a swirl of a skirt and a gauzy white peasant blouse.

Theodor brushed a pale brown feather from her skirt and another from her waistband, then gave her permission to turn back. "The two of you have been busy this week."

"Yes."

"What was it Monday? You visited Waterschloss Anif? And I know you enjoyed it."

"Very much," she said gaily, although she carefully averted direct eye contact with Theodor. Unfortunately, when Rand's grandfather's mind was sharp, he was almost as shrewd as his grandson.

Leigh had more than "enjoyed" the tour of Waterschloss Anif. She'd loved it. A modern-day Cinderella had been filmed at the eleventh-century castle, and the setting was the stuff of romance and fantasy. The place had a wooden bridge guarded by two stone knights, dark dungeons and passageways, a setting of mountains and lakes. The tour had been historically accurate and fascinating. Rand had stolen her off in the middle of it and kissed her. Kissed her silly. Kissed her crazy. Kissed her until . . .

"And Tuesday you were out late," Rand's grandfather prodded her amiably. "I forget where you went now. I think . . . to hear a different kind of music."

"Yes."

"And you liked that, too?"

"Oh, yes," Leigh said blithely, but her mind was spinning back. They'd spent the whole day here— Rand had work to do—but in the evening, he'd taken her to a local wine tavern to hear the *"heurigen* songs" that were uniquely Austrian.

The place was crowded, the music hand-clapping exuberant, the atmosphere brimming with *"gemutlichkeit"*—comradeship and good cheer. They'd served dark beer and wurst and pretzels. It was a place to laugh and have fun. She had. It was only later, when they'd walked to the car, that Rand had pulled her to him. Under a gas streetlight, with fog swirling around their feet, he'd kissed her. Kissed her silly. Kissed her crazy. Kissed her until . . .

Leigh pushed at her hair. A few months ago, she had blown out her birthday candles with a wish in mind—a woman's classic fantasy type of wish—a wish for a month in a foreign land, with a handsome man at her side who romanced and charmed and wooed with a guarantee of no complications.

Her wish had been granted.

Only now she wanted to hang her fairy godmother.

A week ago, Rand had promised that their physical relationship wouldn't cross the line to making love. He had successfully proven his integrity, honor and control, Leigh thought fretfully. In fact, if he proved any more integrity, honor and control, he was going to drive her out of her mind.

Conceivably her falconer thrived on sexual frustration. She doubted it. Granted, she was naive, but even a country-bred, farmer-town miss knew when a knight had taken honor too far. The source of Rand's control was no secret. He'd told her. Until his life changed, until he could offer security and stability, he wouldn't risk a woman's getting hurt in a serious relationship.

It nagged her, that he was wrong. It nagged her like a hangnail. All week, she'd been inseparably part of his life, going out when he had free time, pitching in around here when he didn't. She knew Rand now. In so many ways, he put other people first. In too many ways, he equated doing what was right with denial of his own personal life. *Tackle him, Merrick. It has to be you. So it'll be a little tricky and it'll take some guts, but who's going to do it if you don't?*

"There now," Theodor scolded affectionately. "You've worked a pin loose, and your hair was up so pretty. Let me see if I can help."

His gnarled old fingers awkwardly pushed the hairpin back in just as she heard a chuckle behind her.

"I see you've got your hands on my girl again, Gramps."

Theodor's eyes met hers. "My grandson is," he said gravely, "a bad tease."

"Believe me, I know."

"If I were a few years younger, if I did not have my Renate, I would be the one to take you dancing. You would have a much better time. You would not have to listen to his terrible jokes—"

"She likes my jokes, Gramps."

"She couldn't."

The two kept up a perfectly normal crossfire. No one but Leigh seemed to notice the electric charge smoking up the hall. Midway through the conversation with his grandfather, Rand dropped a fast kiss on her mouth, nothing more than an apologetic sorry-I-took-so-long smack, yet the look in his eyes should have been censored. And while he was still talking, he squeezed her shoulder and set a deliberately rib-hugging, hip-grazing gait for the nearest door.

There was no hope he was going to be good. His smile alone was more illicit than sin. All his body language communicated that he wanted her alone, now, preferably naked and flat, but he'd settle for what he could get. He was a man. She was a woman. And he was going to make damn sure they had a good time.

"Take care of my girl," Herr Krieger called after them.

"The hell I will. I'm going to dance her feet off."

Shooting, Leigh decided, was too good for the scoundrel. She'd have to find another way to take care of Rand—some way to love him, some way to help him—before she disappeared from his life, back to Kansas, and the chance was gone.

* * *

"It won't take us long to get there. At most a half hour."

"You ended up with a long day. You sure you're up for an evening out?" Leigh asked with concern.

"I think an escape is just what the doctor ordered," Rand assured her. Surprising him not at all, though, Leigh let the conversation lag. No matter how upbeat his mood, after a long preoccupying workday he needed a little quiet time to unwind. She always knew, he thought. Like no one else—ever in his life— he could count on Leigh to be accepting, understanding. Restful.

Ahead, the car lights illuminated still meadows and hillsides full of dusky shadows. In the closed car, a hint of perfume teased his nose. When Leigh crossed her legs, he heard the faintest slide of silk—another tease to his senses.

He briefly entertained the fantasy of kidnapping her. Permanently kidnapping her, to some South Sea island where she could tease him for the rest of their natural lives. He'd let her pack the perfume, but no clothes. He'd...

Rand shifted in the seat, his body responding too easily to the mental image of Leigh naked. So much for restful. He groped for any topic that would channel his mind toward safer harbors. "You get on with him like a house afire."

"Your grandfather?" She smiled through half-closed eyes. "That's not hard. He's impossible not to love."

"I'm a little partial to him, too. On his good days. Two days ago I found a fortune in food in the cellars.

Hoarded 'for the war.'" He downshifted for a steep downhill curve, then sneaked in, "I've been waiting forever for you to own up."

"Own up?"

"You two have been keeping secrets. You think I didn't know? He covers for you when you sneak off to the falcons. And I have a feeling you knew where my canned goods were disappearing. Partners in crime, the pair of you."

He heard a very small, very guilty "Whoops." She crossed those lethally silk-clad legs again. "I really should have told you about the food. But at the time, I'd promised him—"

"Hey, it's okay. I was teasing you, not criticizing. He lights up like a Christmas tree whenever you're around." Over the past week, Rand had seen exactly how wonderful she was with his grandfather. He'd wanted to tell her before, wanted to thank her, but a predictable knot of stress tightened in his gut when Gramps was on his mind.

"Rand." She turned her head, leaning her cheek against the velour upholstery, her voice as soothing as salve for a burn. "I know the problem's tough. But that doesn't make him less lovable or loving."

Time to change the subject to the weather. Instead, his palm closed tight on the gearshift, and he heard himself saying, "He's been good for a week, but it's there like a shadow—knowing he could get worse at anytime."

"So if that happens, you do what you have to do," she said gently. "That's really what you've done all along, and from where I'm sitting, no one could possibly handle the problem better than you have."

"Honey, you're dreaming. There are whole days that I know damn well I'm handling nothing well." His tone wasn't sharp, yet Leigh fell silent. It ate at him, that he might have hurt her feelings, so he was stuck explaining. "All I meant was...I miss my home, I miss my family."

He felt her gaze resting on his face, not judging him, not pushing, just...waiting. Before he knew it, a whole lot of baggage slipped the gate that he never meant to talk about at all. All the big things he missed—his three brothers, their families, the job he'd loved—and when he drained that reservoir, Leigh bullied the little stuff out of him, too.

"Tell me," she coaxed.

"It's just stupid things."

"Tell me anyway."

"It's a hell of a silly list." The dusk had deepened into an anonymously black night. "I miss...sitcoms and cop shows. Milkshakes. Barbecues on a hot summer night and sparklers on the Fourth of July. Rush-hour traffic and Tom Brokaw and pizza and McDonald's french fries." He glanced at her, sure she'd laugh.

She didn't. When she gently changed the subject, Rand was relieved. It was like Leigh to be perceptive to his feelings. She always seemed to sense when he was uncomfortable.

Later it would occur to him that at that precise moment, his soft-voiced, blue-eyed, oversensitive innocent was preparing to take him out.

"The other day," she mentioned absently, "your grandfather was telling me about your work here. He gave me a different perspective. I guess you'd call it an environmental perspective.''

"Environmental?"

"Environmental," she echoed. "Like...we have our pollution problems at home, but I'd never considered how much more complicated the issues are in Europe. For one thing, Americans haven't had as many centuries to mess up our environment. For another, here, every bordering neighbor has different politics. Austrians have a long history of loving their woods and wildlife, for instance, but they're stuck sharing rivers, sharing mountains, sharing air—"

"Gramps must have given you quite a lecture."

She responded with a guileless sweet smile—and kept on talking. "So, very obviously, it's harder to save your birds of prey here, harder to protect them. It's not work you can do in a vacuum. In fact, Theodor said you stirred up a real hornet's nest in the beginning, raising a lot of environmental issues that people really didn't want to talk about . . . he said you had to put together your hospital on a real frayed shoestring." Another guileless smile. "That's certainly changed, Rand. Heavens! Right now you have so much work that you're understaffed, stressed for space, and you have the funds to expand. You've obviously convinced more than a few people that you make a difference.''

"Hell. Gramps must have talked your ear off."

And that was when she moved in for the kill. He never saw it coming; how could he? Her eyes were still butter soft, her tone as sweet as honey. "You're not going to leave here so easily, Krieger.''

"I'd leave in two shakes if it weren't for my grandfather," he corrected her.

Leigh didn't argue with him. She just gently rambled on. "No one's suggesting that you give up your country. No one's saying you don't miss your family and home. I just think you might have to accept that you're stuck with the hard road. You have allegiances in two countries. They're not going to disappear."

She let that sink in for several merciless seconds before leaning forward, suddenly—remarkably—all excited and lighthearted and happy. "That huge bonfire up ahead. Is that where we're going? Are we here?"

"We are." Rand parked in the middle of a field. He pocketed the car key, trying to remember when he'd been more furious with a woman. He opened the car door, trying to remember the last time he'd let a woman close enough to hurt him. Rand had told no one, hinted to no one, how hard and lonely the past seven years had been. He'd opened up to Leigh because he knew he could count on her sympathy, her understanding, her compassion.

Instead he got this junk implying it was about time he accepted the choices he'd made and live with them.

He grabbed her hand—even in the parking area, the crowd was thick—and caught Leigh warily sneaking a peak at his face. She should be wary, although he was pretty sure she had no idea what she'd unleashed.

Her little lecture shouldn't have surprised him. If they hadn't known each other long in calendar time, they'd spent almost every waking hour together. He knew Leigh—enough to be certain that she really wasn't shook by the problem of his grandfather. She really wasn't shook by the problem of his allegiance to two countries.

Likely, Rand considered, he should have concluded long ago that the obstacles affecting his commitment to a relationship didn't exist—not with the right woman. He could excuse his lack of insight on the obvious grounds. He'd known a hell of a lot of women.

But none of them had been Leigh.

"Rand?" As soon as he smiled, the wariness disappeared from her eyes. Her fingers tightened trustingly in his. Leigh simply had no idea how much trouble she was in. "It looks a little...wild."

"It's early yet. Believe me, it'll get wilder."

A Romany style music festival was the excuse for the bash. Rand had some doubts there were any authentic gypsies around, but no one in the crowd was going to nitpick that small detail. Colorfully painted wagons edged the field, each selling something—trinkets, fortunes, food and wine. The main action, though, focused around the popping, sparkling bonfire, where couples of all ages were kicking up their heels. The gypsy fiddles were hot, the chords exotic and erotic and primitive.

"Let's just get our bearings for a few minutes," Rand suggested.

Leigh agreed. By the time they'd circled the action, she was wearing a dozen gold bangles on her wrist, a red rose had been tucked in the gathered throat of her blouse, and she'd had her fortune read—tarot cards, then palm. She loved it all, but her eyes—yearning, wistful—kept ricocheting to the dancers.

"Ready to give it a try?" he asked her.

"Rand, I couldn't."

"No?"

Leigh had rarely exposed her shy streak to Rand—she had too much gutsy pride to let the problem get the better of her—but occasionally even strong cookies crumbled. She took another look at the nature of dancing and violently shook her head. She wouldn't, couldn't. The dances were too fast, too wild, the steps nothing she knew. She'd embarrass him. She'd embarrass herself. It was out of the question.

"Okay," Rand said calmly.

One glass of wine had no effect on Ms. Stonewall. After he ruthlessly plied her with a second, her feet started tapping. After glass three, there was just the teeniest crack in her inhibitions. If *he* wanted to dance—only if *he* wanted to dance—she'd try a slow one. But only the slow dances, and only with him.

Three and a half hours later, she had yet to sit down—or let him sit down, either. Fate finally took pity on him when Leigh admitted to a delicate call of nature. Rand figured he'd have at least a five-minute break. Maybe more. He'd never met a woman yet who could resist primping and fussing in a women's rest room.

In three minutes flat, she was back at his side. Right off, he knew something was wrong. Her cheeks were flushed with hectic color—embarrassed color—and though the music was a nominally slow beat, she more or less hurled herself in his arms.

Rand didn't complain. Raised a gentleman, he shielded his lady through the entire slow dance, holding her cheek to cheek and hip to hip. There was no law against teasing a woman beyond the limits of reason, but Austrians could get touchy about public exposure. Maybe it was wisest the tempo changed to something fast. By then, besides, he'd figured out what the problem was.

"I don't think your shadow's going to disappear, honey."

"Shadow?" Her fingers were still wrapped around his neck. She'd forgotten them, and the sleepy look in her eyes did dangerous things to his ego and worse things to his libido—but now wasn't the time to pursue it.

"Shadow," he repeated.

Recognition dawned, regretfully obliterating any trace of passion in her eyes. "Oh, no." Leigh glanced over her shoulder at the soulful-eyed boy who'd followed her from the ladies' room. "Rand, I clearly *told* him no. I *told* him I was with you." To the boy she said firmly, "I'm with him." She poked Rand's chest.

Clearly mortifying Leigh to no end, the young man immediately and earnestly engaged Rand in a quick-paced dialogue in German.

"Good grief. What did he say?"

"I'm not real familiar with his dialect, but the general gist is that your eyes are like stars, your hair is like the gold of the sun, and your figure is to die for." Rand's mouth twitched. "He wants to dance with you." He looked the boy over carefully. "Just one. And he swears on his mother's life that he'll bring you back safely."

"Tell him that I value his mother's life and I think he's very sweet, but no." Leigh listened to the ensuing exchange, but she didn't hear a *"nein."* Her eyes widened. "Rand, did you tell him—hey!"

"Come on. Look at those pitiful eyes. How can you turn him down?" The instant Rand winked permission, the young man snatched Leigh's hand and pulled. He didn't have to yank all that hard. Rand could see Leigh's fingers already snapping to the music, and it was a laughing scold she threw over her shoulder.

"Whatever happened to honor and chivalry? You're supposed to save a damsel in distress, you turkey, not throw her to the wolves—"

Rand wasn't too worried about the damsel in distress routine. The wolf she'd accused him of abandoning her to was barely a cub in training. The boy's admiration was good for her ego—and the break was going to be incomparably good for his feet.

Digging into his pocket for change, he took two full ice waters off a vendor's hands and worked his way through the throng of people. Noises and sounds muted as he climbed the woody hillside, seeking a deserted spot where he could watch in peace and privacy.

The cool grass in a nest of pines fit the bill. He stretched out and drained the first cup of water, but his gaze never left the scene below.

It was long past midnight. The bonfire had diminished to that of an oversize camp fire, and the crowd had started to thin out. Those left were the hard-core, never-say-die music lovers. The firelight illuminated sweat glistening off foreheads and open throats, swirling skirts, and the glint of gold bracelets and hoop earrings. No one had been in shoes for ages, in-

cluding Leigh. Rand had no trouble identifying her in
the crowd. She was the one with the glowing face, the
eyes like sparklers, the hair flying around her like gold
swishy silk.

Rand rubbed an itch near his shoulder blade against
the cool springy grass. The itch, as he should have expected, refused to go away. The hussy with the freckles had worn him out, a relatively simple problem. His
energy level would recover in time.

Any chance of recovering his heart was unlikely.
Falling in love with Leigh, of course, wasn't supposed to happen. There wasn't supposed to be a
ghost's chance, a maiden's prayer, a rain-in-the-desert
possibility of getting hooked.

He was hooked and sinking deeper. It wasn't all his
fault. Daily exposure to Leigh could coax a recalci-
trant whale on a fish hook.

She changed the way he looked at everything—his
life, his situation, his work, his feelings. Beneath her
layer of shyness and inhibitions was a spicy sense of
humor, an exuberance for life, a uniquely woman's
strength. Rand was a fighter by nature. Leigh accepted. Rand lived by rigid, honorable rules about
right and wrong. Leigh, pure female, wasted no time
on judgmental values. When she saw need, she acted.
No pride, no nerves, no terror of rejection would stop
her from taking on a lion in its lair if she thought the
lion were in trouble.

And then there was sex.

Rand leaned back and closed his eyes. He'd kept his
promise to her. They hadn't made love—but not because of any blasted promise. When he had Leigh in

his arms, neither honor nor willpower were worth half a dream.

But her response to him was. Leigh's lack of confidence had an incredible effect on the way she saw herself. His sleeping beauty needed more than kisses to truly wake her... yet when he first kissed her, Leigh had no awareness of the powers she had as a woman. Rand knew that was changing. Every time they came together, he could see her gaining faith in herself— faith in her powers, her rights, her needs.

To rush Leigh, Rand sensed, was to lose her. But to give her a rush was the only weapon he had. Two weeks. That's all they had left. To show her what they could have, might be, together.

He frowned suddenly, leaning forward. Below, the fast-paced gypsy folk dance had ended. The violins had changed to something seductive and slow. And his blonde—so easy to spot in the swarthy-skinned crowd—was nowhere in sight.

Panic rifled through him. Leigh was plenty gutsy when it came to helping someone else, but she didn't have a tough bone in her body. He'd thought the boy's crush would boost her confidence, but by God if that pup had dared to come on to her—

Rand sprang to his feet... only to hear a distinctive huff and puff from the knoll just below him. As dark and shadowed as his cache of pines, the starlight amply illuminated the hillside.

A straggly, tangled gold halo emerged first, followed by a glowing damp face, then a bare shoulder. She'd lost the rose, she'd lost her shoes, she'd lost her hairpins—and he'd never seen a sexier waif. When the evening began, her peasant blouse had been tied at the throat like a nun. No more. Not only was one shoulder exposed, but the strings dangled in front like drunken sailors. As fast as she fanned her hot throat, Rand caught intermittent glances of a delectable pair of hard-heaving lungs.

By the time her feet were on level ground, Rand was leaning lazily back on one elbow. "Will you look at what the cat dragged home?" he drawled.

Eight

"**H**ow could you," Leigh panted, "have done that to me? That boy was a *teenager*. You *know* how much energy and stamina teenagers have. I thought I was going to have a heart attack. Why didn't you come down and save me?"

"Because I thought you were having a great time?"

"That's the most pitiful excuse I've ever heard. If you can't do better than that, Krieger..." She heard the jingling of ice cubes in the tall cup extended toward her. She peered in, then grabbed with both hands. "Okay, okay. Your hero status is restored. I forgive you everything."

"Good thing you're easy to please."

"I was dying for water," she admitted. He watched her throat contract, as gulp after lusty gulp, she upended the cup. She paused only once to catch her breath. "And it's *cold*. I guess I'm going to have to grant you hero status for life. Only how many people did you have to kill to get the ice cubes?"

"No murder required, just the crossing of palms. Although you could probably have had diamonds for the same price." As they both knew, ice cubes were a rarity anywhere in Europe.

"I'm happy with ice water. Forget the diamonds."

"Men dream of hearing a woman say those precious words," he teased, and just managed to catch the cup of leftover ice before it fell. As soon as Leigh caught her breath, she folded next to him like a collapsed slinky, making him grin.

"It may take me a second or two to recover," she confessed.

"I can't imagine why, after nearly four hours of straight dancing."

"Four hours? You're kidding. No wonder I'm so hot." She curled an arm behind her head and nuzzled her back against the cool grass, as completely relaxed as Rand had ever seen her. "I have to admit...I wasn't so sure what we were getting into when we first got here. It's just good fun. At least half the people down there are just plain old families—but you can't imagine what my Aunt Matilda would make of this."

"No?"

"Guzzling wine and pagan dances. And bare feet. Especially the bare feet. She'd see it as a real scene of debauchery."

There was just a tiniest edge to her chuckle. Rand heard it, was tuned to hear it by now. As carefully as a spy working undercover, Leigh avoided any mention of her background. The only exception—and then, only when her guard was down—was a rare reference to the witch. It was impossible for Rand to think of her aunt on any other terms. Whenever Leigh unconsciously mentioned the old biddy, her natural high spirits bottomed out with sobering speed.

Not this time, he thought, and leaned closer, determined that nothing and no one—even witches—was going to take down her mood tonight. Shadows shifted in the night breeze, but his pupils had long acclimated to the darkness. He could see her. She'd had such a good time, and it showed. Her eyes still had the sparkle of exhilaration, her skin was still glowing. "Are you still thirsty?"

She shook her head. "I'm fine now."

"There's still ice."

"Sounds good." She raised on an elbow and extended her hand, obviously expecting him to hand her the cup.

Instead he dived for the last of the melting ice cubes. Holding one between two fingers, he brushed it across her forehead. Leigh yelped, then laughed, then . . . stopped laughing.

Excitement, like a sleepy cat, lazily stretched its velvet claws. He saw it in her eyes. He'd seen it when he held her in the embrace of every love song. He'd seen it when she finally worked up the terrible courage to tango, to swish and sway with just a hint of recklessness, to grow bolder yet and even dare invite with a sultry smile.

Surrounded by dozens of people, of course, she'd been as safe as a nun in church.

There wasn't a soul around on the pine-shadowed hillside.

He rubbed the cube against her cheek, feeling her eyes rivet to his in the darkness. The scents of pine and grass had never struck him as erotic before. They did now. He trailed the ice down her throat, over the pulse bobbing so fast, and she tensed—but not from the shock of the cold. His lady had just discovered that she was no longer feeling safe.

He sailed the last of the cube along the gathered rim of her peasant blouse, faithfully following the swell of her breast, the dip of her cleavage, the next swell, the rise to her moonlit shoulder. Her knees clapped together. A sough of breath escaped her lips.

"Rand."

"Hmm?"

"I'm not sure . . . what you're doing."

"No? You were overwarm. I'm helping you cool off." He watched a single water droplet, glistening like a diamond, rivel down between her breasts. She shivered suddenly, yet her cheeks flushed with the luster of heat.

"You're not helping me cool off. And you know it. And anyone could come up here."

"Does that worry you?" he murmured.

"Yes." Her eyes said no. Her eyes said she wouldn't notice if a trampling herd of elephants appeared by a miracle on this particular Austrian hillside.

Below, the music had stopped several minutes before. The hour was late; the group began breaking up and closing shop. No one had a reason to head up the hillside; the cars were all parked in the opposite direction. But like Leigh said, someone could. And knowing that someone could was how Rand figured he'd hold on to his sanity.

He dug two fingers into the cup, and came up with the last ice cube. He poked it between her parted lips.

And then he kissed her. Likely Leigh didn't realize that her instinctive reaction was Pavlovian: as soon as his mouth aimed for hers, her arms wrapped around his neck. It had taken him dozens of kisses, hours of kisses, to teach her that basic response. Trust had been hard to win from Leigh.

Trusting anyone but himself had always come hard for Rand. Except with her. His tongue sneaked between her lips. He sought the chip of ice, found it, stole it back. It was smaller, but it tasted like her by then.

"Rand..."

She was trying to think of another objection, but her voice was weak. An alto fast losing its battery. His tongue pushed the cube back to her lips. Leigh liked it, the contrast of damp warm tongues and ice-numbed lips. It drove him to find something she liked much more.

Her breasts were straining, full and white, over the perilously loose neckline of her blouse, and Leigh made a sound. A soft sound, a wild sound when he dipped his head. His beard brushed the shadow between the cleft, and his tongue licked a drop of moisture. He tasted salt. He tasted the texture and scent of Leigh. She could be unbearably sensitive around her breasts.

So could he. Shifting an inch lower, he cupped both rounded orbs between his palms. The material of her blouse was gauzy thin; beneath it her bra was a smooth silk. Even through both layers of fabric, he easily found the taut cherry tips. He dampened each with his

tongue, nipped each with the rough tenderness of a
lion for his lioness.

She liked the roughness. She liked the tenderness.
So much so that her fingers found his, clutched his,
dragged his hand to the dangling strings that held her
blouse together. He understood. Bare was better; she
wanted the blouse gone.

For Leigh to dare express even the smallest sexual
demand was such a vulnerable milestone that his
throat went dry. She'd crossed a line—for him, with
him—and he rewarded her with the tenderest of kisses.

A mistake. It seemed she'd lost interest in tender
kisses. Her mouth moved under his, as hot as a sting
and trembling moist. Her slim hands clutched and
kneaded the length of his spine like restless kitten
claws. One hand—for the first time—strayed to his
waist, then below. Or tried to.

He caught her sweet wrist, feeling sweat bead on his
forehead. Desire shot through him, potent and powerful and hammering hot. There was no chance in hell
he could keep his head if she touched him, and suddenly he wanted—needed—every ounce of control.

He wrapped his arms around her, tight, and pushed
them both into motion. He rolled her on top of him,
then beneath him, then deeper in the shadows. Startled and breathless, she laughed, sure he was playing.

He wasn't. When he slid a hand up her bare thigh,
the yards of her skirt concealed his intent. From any
chance stranger, not from Leigh.

Her eyes flew open, fastened on his face. The smile
faded from her mouth. Her lips softened, then parted
on a tremulous breath. She was wearing tap pants in a
satin so slippery they could drive a man crazy.

Watching every nuance of expression on her face, he pushed them down over the rounded curve of her hip, meshed his fingers through her silky curling hair and cupped her.

A riplike tear knifed through his whole body. She was already warm, already wet. For him.

Tension vibrated between them, not playful now, but an urgent, hungry rush. He fueled it, with a hot wet kiss that started on her lips and ended with his mouth buried in her throat. Below, he cupped and released her in a rhythm older than time, his thumb circling the bud that was too sensitive to touch.

"Rand—" She called his name. And again. They'd never been this far before, she knew. Tonight was different. She sensed that, too. Excitement had exploded between them before, but relinquishing control was a far more dangerous intimacy. Tonight he wanted her to feel that danger. The danger, the power, the pleasure.

Her body told him secrets that he wanted to know, needed to know to make that happen. He'd guessed she was a virgin or the same as. Now he knew. No matter how moist and ready she was, even a single finger stretched her delicate, tight sheath. Two fingers risked the border between pleasure and pain.

She wanted two.

She demanded two, with her eyes and her hands and a breaking cry like a whisper on the wild.

Her legs flexed and her throat arched, bare and brazen for the lick of his tongue. Her small hands roped around his neck again. She couldn't hold on any tighter if he were a life raft in a stormy ocean. He took her over the edge, cushioning her cry with his mouth, absorbing the spiral of heat and spasm of sweet, sweet pleasure that shook all through her.

When it was over, he was breathing harder than she was. She lay limp, her cheek buried in the hollow of his shoulder. So precious, she felt. So right. Most unwillingly, he withdrew his hand, caressing the round of her hip and the soft flesh of her belly before gently adjusting her clothes. He kissed her brow and cradled her close again, well aware the night temperature was dropping and the grass becoming sticky with dew. They couldn't stay much longer, but he'd be damned if he was capable of letting her go yet.

Eventually Leigh lifted her head, offering a close-up snapshot of all the damages he'd wrought. Her lips looked swollen, her cheeks whisker-burned, and her hair tangled, like crushable silk, around his fingers. It was her eyes that took him out the most, though. They were as dark as navy by moonlight and naked with emotion—stunned wonder and a delectable shyness and something as dark and soft and complex as love.

Rand felt her love as sure as he breathed.

Though Leigh might not believe it, what just happened between them had nothing to do with sex, and everything to do with sabotage. Ruthless sabotage. Desperate men did desperate things, and unfortunately he wanted all of Leigh or nothing. He was too old, too smart—and too damn scared of losing her—to play for small stakes.

His sleeping beauty would have him believe that she'd been asleep for a hundred years before their first kiss. That was hooey. Rand wasn't worried about the "secrets" in her life—he knew everything about Leigh that he needed to know. She was strong, loving and loyal, perceptive and smart—but she didn't believe any of that.

Using sex was dishonorable sabotage, yet Rand saw no other way to teach her confidence. Whenever they touched, she was honest, open, real. He wanted, reveled in, Leigh newly discovering her powers as a woman, but that was only half the mountain. She trusted him. What he wanted—needed for her, for them—was for Leigh to trust her own feelings.

They wouldn't make love until she did.

Even if he died of sexual frustration. Which, at the moment, struck him as a distinctly real possibility.

"Krieger," she said gently.

"Yeah?" God, he loved it when she called him Krieger. She only did it when she was really shook, really determined to handle something she was positive she couldn't.

"We have a problem here," Leigh said tactfully. Her eyes met his, then dropped faster than weighted lead. She focused on his cheek and her voice was a little breathy, but she was going to build her bridge over the River Kwai no matter what the odds. "The problem is that I can never predict what you're going to do."

"I'm sorry."

"You should be. You're in trouble. Very bad trouble with me." She tugged at his beard, as if determined to catch his attention. She already had his complete, undivided and astute attention. Such a look on her face. Rand had the sneaky suspicion that the schoolmarm was about to teach the class jock the more embarrassing facts of life. "You knew. You knew, Krieger, that here, now, tonight in these woods, that we couldn't possibly..."

"True." He saved her from having to spell it out.

"So you also knew that if you started something, any...um...mutual activity would be risky. If not impossible."

"True." It was starting to be the best lecture he'd ever had.

"You started it anyway."

"True."

"Which has happened before. Maybe not like this. But it's definitely happened before."

"True."

With her right breast nestled to his chest, still igniting his libido, and with her legs twined with his, still risking his sanity, she delivered her punchline. "It's one thing to be generous, Rand. It's another to volunteer for the Twilight Zone. And I'm just telling you. We're not putting you through this again."

Maybe, to earn another lecture like this, he could handle dying from sexual frustration another hundred times. He loved the possessive "we," and the bulldog tilt to her chin, and the way she sneaked up on him with humor. He loved *her*.

But he had less than two weeks to convince her that she felt the same way. Anxiety churned in his stomach. Leigh was brave at taking risks—for him. The only risk he wanted—needed—her to take was for herself. And until she was willing to do that, he wasn't going to risk losing her by having her guess there was any other ante on the table but sex. He said gently, "Did you forget? I made you a promise."

"What if..." She hesitated. Her vulnerable heart was in her eyes. "What if I released you from that promise?"

It wasn't every day she offered to sleep with a man. It wasn't every day the man turned her down, took her home, and then spent twenty minutes kissing her at the door as though he'd die if he couldn't have her.

Leigh paced the horseshoe space around her counterpane bed for the dozenth time. It was the ungodly hour of three o'clock in the morning. Everyone in the inn was asleep. Hautberg was asleep. Likely all of Austria and Europe were asleep. Not her.

Rand had said, "There is no way I would break a promise, honey. Not unless I was sure it was right for you."

Well, fine, she kept telling herself. But it wasn't. A rejection she would have understood. Hells bells, she'd been waiting for a rejection ever since she met Rand.

Only every time she replayed his words in her head, she heard no rejection. She heard a knight saving his lady. She heard "I won't have you hurt." She heard Rand's physical—and emotional—denial of his own needs because that was the kind of stupid code of honor he lived by.

It was Leigh's thoughtful opinion that the right woman—a strong, secure, sexually experienced and loving woman—would wrap that code of honor around his neck and strangle time. After dragging him off to bed.

Likely she was going hoot-owl crazy, because she could actually imagine herself in that scenario. The loving part would be so easy. The "strong, secure and sexually experienced'' part was a complete joke, but something *did* happen whenever they were together. Something happened to her, something incredible and wonderful and powerful, something—she was afraid—that was one of the more embarrassing repercussions of falling in love with him.

Sometimes, when she was with Rand, she had the feeling that she could do absolutely anything.

Get real, Merrick.

But just tonight, she couldn't seem to. Her heart was revved up faster than a hot-rod engine; there was no chance of sleeping. After pacing the U-shaped space around the counterpane bed another time, she determinedly pulled on her robe, plugged her bare feet into slippers, and grabbed her leather purse.

The purse-and-pajamas ensemble leaned toward bizarre, but no one would know. The only sound in the whole place was a boarder's muffled snore at the end of the hall. Clutching her purse, she tiptoed downstairs.

The inn was spooky dark—Frau Stehrer was parsimonious about electricity after midnight—but Leigh was afraid of waking anyone with a light. Enough moonlight streamed through the windows that she could distinguish shapes and shadows. The lobby led into a living room/parlor with heavy furniture and a television and claw-footed tables strewn with magazines for the guests. Just beyond the living room was a closet about the size of a telephone booth—which was what it was.

Leigh squeezed into the claustrophobic space and closed the door before reaching for the light string. The bald light bulb glared in her eyes, as she dived into her leather bag for first her phrase book and then her change purse.

The need to call home had hit her as hard as a fast-moving freight train. It didn't matter if the conversation never got heavier than the weather. She just wanted to talk to someone from home. Someone from Kansas. Someone who knew Leigh Merrick, the staid and reliable librarian, the Leigh who had never done anything foolish in her entire life.

The woman she didn't seem to be anymore.

Frau Stehrer had helped her place her one and only transatlantic call—Aunt Matilda had wanted to know if she arrived safely—but it couldn't be that tough to do it alone.

Before picking up the receiver, she dumped all the change on the tiny ledge by the phone. Austrian shillings came in four denominations, and shillings divided into groschens, which also came in four denominations. But not the same denominations. And none of them had ever made a lick of sense to Leigh, but she firmly tucked the phone between her ear and shoulder.

It would be all right. Surely the operator would help her? And her trusty phrase book had pages covering tourist problems like this. She dialed, then reeled off like a true Austrian pro, *"Ich mochte ein Ferngesprach nach* Matilda Silverthorn *machen."*

And the horror began. The operator, although polite and patient, seemed to think Leigh was speaking Russian. *"Ich Verstehe nicht"*—I don't understand—was her persistent response. It took endless frustrating minutes to master the communication problem, and then she heard the obvious instruction to *"bitte, münzen einzahlen."* Fork over the coins. The operator told how much, only translating that from the ledgeful of change was another crisis.

The whole experience was dreadful, yet her mood only grew more buoyant. The money problem was easily solved—she simply fed the pay phone everything she had—and then waited impatiently while the phone rang. The rocky feeling that she wasn't the same person who'd left Kansas was basic silliness. She was still Leigh. It was just going to feel good to catch a little reinforcement and support from home, to touch base with a familiar Kansas voice.

Her aunt's voice crackled over the distance, so strident that Leigh almost jumped. "What's wrong that you're calling so late?"

"Late? I know it's after nine, but I didn't think you'd be in bed yet—"

"I'm not in bed, but you should be. It's after three there. What's wrong that you're up so late?"

Nothing's wrong. For the first time in my life, everything is right. I love him. I know every reason I shouldn't. I know every reason I can't. but when we're together...

"Nothing's wrong," Leigh said cheerfully. "I just wanted to call at a time when I was sure you'd be in, find out how you are and if you're doing okay—"

"You're in trouble, gal. I can hear it in your voice."

Yes, I'm in trouble. The best trouble I've ever had. You can't imagine how I feel when I'm with him. Crazy and wild and open. Open and free like I never imagined I could be with a man...

"I watered your plants and took care of your infernal cats, vacuumed. Had to vacuum. There was cat hair everywhere."

Leigh closed her eyes. "Aunt Matilda, you know you didn't have to do that. I hired Jane to come over every day—"

"She's just a teenager. She doesn't know anything about proper housekeeping. As bad as my arthritis is—"

He makes me feel loved, Aunt Matilda. Loved and wanted and needed, and I don't care if I get hurt. Do you hear me? I don't care. I can't stand it that he's alone. He needs to laugh. He needs to be loved. It seems so simple when we're together....

"Well, have you been sick from the food? Diarrhea?"

Leigh slicked back her hair and squeezed her eyes closed again. She'd obviously caught her aunt in a raw mood. Did it have to matter? "I haven't been sick, and honestly, the food is wonderful here."

"You haven't been drinking the water, have you? And you've been to church?"

"Yes, I've been to church," Leigh said quietly. She could feel it—the surge of buoyant confidence puncturing like a slowly deflating balloon. It wasn't that she ever expected to share her feelings about Rand. Those were private. It was just that there seemed to be nothing she could share with her aunt. Not without sounding half crazy.

"Attending church will help you get over those foolish notions of yours."

Leigh rubbed her forehead with two fingers. From the start, her aunt had labeled her wish to visit Austria's a "foolish notion." "Come on," she said coaxingly. "Everyone needs a vacation. I hadn't been anywhere in years—"

Her aunt harrumphed. "Years past when I needed a vacation, I used the time to clean the cupboards and weed the garden. Nor did I pay anyone to take care of my responsibilities. Joe asked about you." Leigh could hear the sniff clear across the Atlantic. "The orphanage barely had enough volunteers to put on their May fund-raiser. First time you left them in the lurch, gal. Some of us used to remember to help others in less fortunate shoes."

Guilt wrapped around Leigh, as sticky as a spider web. It had always been her life, helping little ones.

"I suppose you've met some man."

Leigh swallowed hard. "Would it be so unforgivable if I had?"

"The only unforgivable thing is for a thirty-year-old grown woman to have delusions about herself and her place in life."

When Leigh hung up the phone, she yanked the string on the light cord and stood in the darkness.

So much, she thought dryly, for any helpful support from Kansas.

Nine

———

The next morning, Leigh was halfway through showering when she heard a knock on the bathroom door. She raised her eyes to the ceiling. "I'll be quick," she called out.

Most of the boarders were up and gone this late. Leigh had assumed, just for once, that she could take her time. Not that it mattered, she told herself as she flicked off the tape and grabbed a towel. Five straight hours in the shower wouldn't likely wake her up anyway. Not this morning.

The knock sounded again. *"Bitte,"* she called. "Two more minutes."

A rash promise when her fingers were all thumbs. Makeup could wait, but she didn't feel comfortable traipsing around in her robe when the other boarders were awake. So she dressed, but it was tricky to button her rose silk blouse and towel dry her hair at the same time. Stockings didn't want to pull over still damp calves. Her skirt zipper caught on a thread, then the belt fought her. Aunt Matilda would have said, "Haste makes waste, gal. When are you going to learn?"

The towel flopped over Leigh's eyes. Since their phone conversation, there was simply no getting her aunt out of her mind. A dozen times, she'd reminded herself that she was thirty now, not twelve. She'd been crushable as a girl, easily shattered with the right word, but it had been ages—years—since she'd let her aunt get to her. As Leigh well knew, Matilda could have a good heart, but catch her at a wrong moment and harshness was simply her way.

Still, her aunt's stab that she had "delusions about herself and her place in life" had shaken her. Hadn't she already accused herself of being a faker? A new hairstyle and some face paint only changed the outside layer. Who was she really but a small-town librarian who'd entertained the grandiose notion that a world-traveled, good-looking, too-damned experienced rogue could actually want her? Actually need her. Even actually *love* her.

In a mood lower than a worm, Leigh pushed her feet into shoes and hurriedly ran the towel around the mirror's steamed edges. *I know you, Merrick. When you offered to sleep with him, you weren't thinking a fast roll. You were thinking love. You were thinking babies and forevers. You were thinking stupid. And as of this instant, your heart's grounded until it behaves itself. You hear me?* Knuckles rapped on the door for a third time. "Good grief," she muttered. It had to be the old gentleman in Room 4. He was always impatient.

She swooped her night gear and toothbrush and shower paraphernalia into the damp towel, blew her drying bangs out of her eyes and whipped open the door.

"Rand!" Shock was the only reason her grounded heart was suddenly thumping so hard.

"Morning, honey." Rand pushed away from the wall and bent down. As if the night had never existed, as if they'd never been apart, he cuffed her neck and dropped a kiss on her perspiration-damp lips. "I missed you."

It was a diabolical, subversive thing to say to a woman clinging tight to a pitch-black mood, and the kiss was more bad news. He tasted...familiar, like the man who'd taken her to the height of intimacy the night before, the one who made her feel as though she could do anything on earth when she was with him.

He tasted like magic, and even when he let her go, the nasty emotion lingered. "You could hardly miss me. We just saw each other seven hours ago."

"That long?" He loped his arms loosely around her shoulders when he lifted his head. He was dressed casually in a leather jacket, white sweater and jeans, and his grin was easy, teasing. "No wonder I was miserable." He looked her over with the greedy scrutiny of the devil for a sinner. Any fool could see that her hair was straggly, her freckles bare, the circles under her eyes bigger than boats. He said, "I think I guessed you'd look terrific even first thing in the morning."

They said love was blind, but Leigh was smart enough to credit the dim light in the hall. "Did you wake up this full of pepper and vinegar, or was it something you had for breakfast? And I could have sworn you promised to sleep in this morning."

"Couldn't sleep in. I had work to do."

"You're not getting any work done if you're here."

"True. But I couldn't do that anyway because I need to talk with you."

Possibly he did, but at that precise moment he was having an incredibly good time knocking her for six. She was *trying* not to love him, but his eyes were full of sass and dance, his pagan beard framed an unholy grin, and she had the terrible suspicion that another kiss was coming unless she did something, quick. She whisked a frantic glance down the hall. "Rand...I know it's the twentieth century, but I'm not at all that sure Frau Stehrer was born in this particular time period. It might make her nervous to find you up here—"

"We wouldn't want to make her nervous," he agreed promptly, with just the slightest stress on the "her." "It'd be much better if we talked in your bedroom." That wasn't quite what she had in mind, but he'd already scooped up her bundled towel. "First door off the stairway, right?"

Apparently it was a rhetorical question since he was already halfway there. By the time she caught up, he was entrenched inside. Like a perfect gentleman, he left the door ajar, dropped her rolled-up towel on a chair, and stuffed his hands into his pockets as if to guarantee they'd behave. He gave her his best trustworthy Boy Scout grin.

Leigh sighed. "It had to be something you had for breakfast. Maybe a mickey in your orange juice?"

"Hmm?"

He wasn't paying attention. He was too busy being curious. Although his hands stayed in his pockets, he prowled the room like a maurauding knight in a medieval virgin's lair. Initially Leigh was amused, because there was absolutely nothing to see. Anything embarrassing with lace or straps was put away—she'd always been hopelessly tidy—and the white counterpane spread neatly covered the bed.

But he didn't once glance at the bed. He glanced at the delicate pearl earrings on her dresser. He glanced at the tiny swan in Austrian crystal that she hadn't been able to resist from a local shop. He glanced at the water glass by her bed, filled with fragile lilies of the valley—a block down, a street vendor sold them fresh each day.

And then he glanced at her, in a way that made her feel all shivery, all female, all . . . exposed. "He sells blood-red roses, too. But they wouldn't appeal to you half as much, would they, honey?"

Rand's voice was gentle and soothing and Leigh didn't like it. He calmed down his falcons the same way—just before he put on their hood. She had the oddest premonition that she'd be a lot safer if he'd found blood-red roses and slinky garter belts and a come-hither negligee lying around.

She crossed her arms across her chest, thinking that she was wrongly interpreting his actions—again. Rand liked to flirt. Rand liked to tease. He'd also proved a thousand times that she was completely safe with him. "Krieger, you said you had to talk to me—"

"I do. About our trip to Vienna."

"*What* trip to Vienna?"

"The two-day trip I'd like to take you on next week." He shifted her towel so he could sprawl in the only bedroom's chair. "If it were my choice, we'd be going this week, not your last. But I can't put it together quite that quickly, and even then I'll need some help from you."

"Rand—" Her heart took in "two days alone with Rand" and "Vienna." Her head flashed *think Aunt Matilda. Think no. Think how deep you're already in.* "You can't leave your grandfather."

"Actually Gramps is the one who insists. You can't leave the country without seeing Vienna, honey. If you even tried, he'd probably go into a decline. I know you wouldn't want that." An edge of a peach lace nightgown peeked out from the towel. "Is this yours?"

She snatched it and calmly whisked it under the bed. "Rand—"

"Janette's staying overnight on the weekdays now, and I've lined up a couple of his cronies to keep an eye on him. He's not a problem, but there are a lot of things to do and see. Some of them have to be arranged ahead, so I thought we'd talk them over starting with breakfast. I don't know about you, but I could use some hot, strong coffee and *pfannkuchen....*"

He let the word *"pfannkuchen"* roll slowly off his tongue—not easy to do in German. He knew how she felt about that particular Austrian delicacy. He *knew.*

Rand crossed his legs at the ankles, lazy, as though he planned to spend the day in her chair if that's what it took. "And then I thought—a horseback ride in the mountains. There's a place I want to show you where a car can't make it. A valley with a mountain pool.

I've seen swans on it. Black swans. You ever see a black swan, honey? I thought we'd take a picnic lunch—it's a good, quiet place to talk." He lifted her tiny crystal swan to the window and squinted at the prisms it reflected.

So did Leigh. In the rainbow prisms, she saw swans on a mountain lake; she smelled the food from a picnic feast; she heard a man's throaty laugh. Rand's laugh—not the flirt's wicked chuckle she'd heard when she first knew him, but the natural belly laugh that came out of him now. They were good together. A cocoon of two. Leigh felt good for him, knowing she'd bullied him into sharing his feelings, and God knew he'd been good for her. Better than good. Wonderful, unforgettable, unbearably special.

And she thought no. Maybe an afternoon in the mountains, but not a two-day trip alone. I just can't afford to fall any more in love with you, Krieger. I'll be going back to Kansas in shambles as it is. So she said, "You have your work. You can't just leave."

"I know."

"It's not that I don't want to go, Rand, but I understand how hard it would be for you."

"It'll take some doing," he admitted.

"It's probably impossible."

"You're probably right," Rand immediately concurred. "The most we could possibly do is talk about it."

She hesitated.

"There's no harm in just talking about it, is there, honey?"

She hesitated again. "No, of course not."

"Of course not," he echoed, as soft as a murmur.

* * *

Rand checked his watch as he pushed open the hotel room door. It was 6:10.

He dropped his overnighter just inside and hung up his suit and tux with a cursory glance at the room. Typical of old Vienna, the furnishings were baroque—the night tables marble, the chairs upholstered in brocade, and the headboard for the king-size bed gilt-gold. A little sissy for his tastes, but Leigh liked old stuff. He noted the connecting door. Downstairs, checking in, Leigh had so obviously expected to have the room on the other side. Instead he'd reserved her room at the opposite end of the long, long hall.

He wasn't giving her any excuse to be nervous.

They had agreed to meet in an hour—enough time to get settled, catch a shower and change clothes before dinner. The drive had been long, and traffic was heavy once they neared Vienna. Every tense muscle in his body craved a quick hot soak, but he glanced at his watch again—6:14.

There were no guarantees in life, but Rand was pretty sure he was going to be interrupted in a matter of minutes. He postponed the shower. Rolling his shoulders to get the kinks out, he crossed to the window.

Vienna was below. At the foot of the alpine ranges, cradled on the Danube River, some said she was the heart of Europe. Most urban centers were tough. Not Vienna. She was delicate spired cathedrals and cut crystal and the best of wines. She was style and grace and elegance. She'd always protected the gentle people—artists of the canvas, like Klimt and Schiele; art-

ists of the intellect like Freud; artists of music, like
Mozart and Schubert and Brahms. Vienna had sheltered culture through the centuries as fiercely as any
wolf dam guarded her vulnerable cubs. She'd also
sheltered lovers. Vienna always had been, always
would be, a magic city for lovers.

Rand needed that magic to work on Leigh, because
when he looked below, what he really saw was Cus-
ter's Last Stand.

He cupped the aching tense muscles at the back of
his neck. Her plane left for the States in three short
days. There was an acrid, sharp taste in his mouth that
was becoming familiar. The taste was damn close to
desperation.

He'd lied to Leigh—he could easily have taken her
to Vienna anytime in the last week. Instead he'd made
the deliberate choice to keep her home, by his side,
because home was real life and it was in real life that
he wanted to prove to Leigh that they belonged together.

God knew, he thought he had. She fit him, every
way, everywhere, whether he was working with his
falcons or handling his grandfather, whether they were
traipsing the woods or bumping hips in the kitchen.
She unraveled his head, every damn time he touched
her. She unraveled his soul, every time she gutsily took
him on, all vulnerable heart and love naked in her
eyes, the confidence of a waif and so damned stubborn he could wring her neck.

He could woo that woman from here to high hell.
But he couldn't make her believe she was loved. Not
when she saw herself as unlovable.

A staccato rap sounded at the door. Then another,
more frantic, forcing him to smile. "Coming," he

called. A total lie. Taking his own sweet time, he pushed off his shoes, mussed his hair and tugged his shirt loose from his pants.

A small fist pounded on the door, arguably loud enough to wake the dead. He wiped off his grin and sedately strolled for the door. The knob was barely turned before the whirlwind catapulted inside. Obviously the poor baby hadn't planned on going calling just then, because her feet were bare, her hair skewed up and damp from a bath, and almost every button mismatched on her jeweled print dress. His brows raised in shocked surprise. "Heavens. What's wrong?"

"You know what's wrong. You know exactly what's wrong. And you're probably the most crazy man I've ever met in my entire life—"

"Sweetheart, I don't have the least idea what you're talking about."

"Then I'll *show* you exactly what I'm talking about—"

"Hold on there. I don't have any shoes on."

"Forget the shoes, Krieger." She grabbed his hand and yanked it. Obediently he allowed himself to be marched down the hall, past the elevators, and past the turn. Only one room door was standing wide open, where she stopped dead, her breasts heaving in agitation as she jerked her head. "Go on. Look," she ordered him.

"Honey, you really should have locked your door—"

"*Krieger.*"

So he peered in, although there was nothing he hadn't expected to see. Leigh's room was identical to

He'd taken her to see the old masters at the Museum of Fine Arts, then to see the new masters in Belvedere Palace. He'd dragged her shopping, heaping her arms with treasures—enamel earrings, an antique music box, a crystal falcon, a threaded gold shawl...good grief, she didn't dare look at anything before he was reaching for it.

And then there was food. He seemed to develop a terror of her being hungry. He'd fed her pretzels and beer on the banks of the Danube, *wienerschnitzel* in one of the cozy pubs the locals called Beisel, and plied her with Vienna's specialties—pastries and chocolates. There was no reasoning with the man. None. He got this caveman look in his eyes if he thought there was something she wanted, and any attempt to argue with him resulted in no mercy.

In a few short blocks, they reached the hotel. Rand paid the driver and threaded her through the gilt-edged revolving doors to the lobby. "How does a nightcap sound?"

"Terrific." She automatically turned toward the small intimate bar at the far end of the lobby, but Rand grabbed her hand.

"Let's have it upstairs. It'll be more relaxing, and I know you're beat."

Her gaze riveted to his face. "Sure." He strode off to arrange room service from the desk clerk, leaving her heart hammering and her toes squeezed together. The reaction kicked in the moment Rand mentioned "upstairs"—although heaven knew why. Last night he'd left her at her door after the shortest kiss in their personal history.

Stepping into the elevator with him a few minutes later, Leigh fidgeted with an earring, fussed with her purse strap and smiled like mad. She had no excuse for being so miserable. At least on the subject of chemistry, Rand's behavior was only logical. She was leaving Austria in less than two days. Rand was a man who kept his promises, and withdrawal from the closeness they'd shared was simply being sensible.

When the elevator reached the seventh floor, she said logically and sensibly, "Your room or mine?"

The smallest smile tugged the corner of his mouth. "Yours," he said easily, and dug her key out of his pocket. He still didn't trust her with keys. With his hand at the small of her back, he led her down the hall, opened her door and flicked on the overhead.

Her heart dropped another three feet. Closed up all these hours, the room smelled hopelessly of edelweiss—not an overpowering perfume, but the tease of mountain meadows and sun-drenched hills and memories. The tease of a man she was never going to have. The tease of the only man she'd ever really wanted. The tease of the man she was in love with. Stop it, Merrick.

Rand negotiated all the pots to ease into the carved brocade armchair by the bed. "I didn't think they'd last this long."

"They're not cut, they're potted. I don't think a wildflower would have lasted otherwise—they're wonderful, Rand."

"Yeah, I thought you'd like them."

She couldn't wait any longer to push off her shoes. Her aching toes and arches sank into the deep pile carpet. At least her feet were going to live. Until that moment she hadn't been sure.

She'd just dropped her evening bag on the bureau when there was a knock. Both sprang for the door at the same time. The bellboy looked startled at his enthusiastic reception.

The boy pulled in a two-tiered cart. On the top shelf, two snifters of warm brandy sat on a tray. When Rand slipped the boy a bill, though, Leigh noticed that the bottom shelf held an odd basin-shaped pot covered with a starched white cloth.

The boy lugged it into the room—it was obviously heavy—and at Rand's direction, set it on the carpet at the foot of her bed. "What's this?" she asked as soon as they were alone again.

"Hot water and baby oil."

She blinked. "For what on earth?"

Rand chuckled . . . a throaty chuckle that struck her as the first honest, natural laugh she'd heard from him in two days. "For your feet. You've been walking around on those spindles for hours, and I wore you out walking the whole day before that. Don't tell me those toes couldn't use a soak."

"Rand—" It was the kind of unbearable kindness and consideration he'd shown her since they arrived in Vienna. "I don't believe you did this."

"I don't believe you're still standing there in those stockings—unless you plan to soak them, too."

So she peeled off her stockings in the bathroom, and came back in the sexiest black dress she'd ever owned and bare feet. He handed her the warmed brandy as she sat on the edge of the bed. She took the first sip at

the same time her tortured, weary, aching feet dipped
into the warm water.

"I'm gonna die."

"Feels that good, hmm?"

"You can't imagine." Her eyes flew to his. "Believe me, I'm not complaining. I wanted to go absolutely everywhere we went. I've loved every
minute—"

"It's just that your feet aren't used to walking
ninety miles a day?"

"Exactly." Her toes, malfunctional for hours,
started wiggling. Her arches, cramped and tight,
loosened in the silky warm water. "This is heaven.
Maybe better than."

"Good," Rand murmured. He lifted his brandy
snifter, gulped down the few swallows and stood up.
"Unfortunately we have a long travel day ahead of us
tomorrow."

"Pardon?"

"You just enjoy. I won't stay— I know you need to
unwind and relax." He bent down and cocked his
head. She saw blue eyes, silver blue and glinting like
hard metal, coming toward her. She felt his lips, com-
pressed and cool, brush against hers. She saw a smile
lift away from her that was as stark as a desert. "I'll
see you in the morning, honey."

"Rand—"

He winked at her, and then he was gone. The door
clicked closed. Leigh sat frozen in surprise. She was
still holding the brandy. Her bare feet were still ankle
deep in the incredibly soothing oil-scented water. The
oil-scented water that Rand had ordered, because he
guessed her feet were sore, the same way he'd intuited

her every need since coming to Vienna. Longer than Vienna, she mentally corrected herself. Since the first rotten day she'd landed in Austria.

There was no sound in the room. Certainly no sound remotely resembling the cock of a gun and the snapped jerk of a safety being removed.

But the water noisily sloshed when Leigh lifted her dripping feet. "I'll be damned if you're going to get away with this, Krieger. Double damned. Triple damned. I've had *enough*."

Ten

Leigh left soaking footprints en route to the door, tugged it open, and dripping straight down hall. Already Rand was out of sight. Frustratingly hampered by her long straight skirt, she hiked it to her knees. A dowager in mauve chiffon exited the elevator, trailed by three bellboys and a cartful of luggage. They all got an eyeful of her lickety-split race down the hall in bare feet, but she didn't care. When she reached Rand's room, she pounded on the door.

The door opened a crack, then angled wide. At a glance, she could see that his shirttails were hanging and the buttons all undone. He hadn't wasted a single second getting comfortable. "Leigh—Honey, what's the matter?"

She heard the kindly solicitous tone—again. And blew. "Don't you honey me, Rand Krieger." She poked his chest, forcing him in, and closed the door

with her foot—hard enough to make a resonant slam.
"I'm sick sick sick of it."

"Sick of—"

"Sick of your being nice. Sick of your being sweet.
Sick of your being considerate. For cripes' sakes, what
is the *matter* with you?"

Rand paused—no longer than the beat of her
heart—and then calmly lifted his hand to flick off the
glaring overhead. With only the soft glow of the bedside lamp behind him, his expression was shadowed.
"I'm not sure I understand, but maybe if you run that
past me again. Something must be the matter with me
because I've been kind and considerate to you?"

He said it so gently, with such cautious humor, that
she never noticed the odd watchfulness in his face. She
blew the hair out of her eyes and propped her fists on
her hips. "I'm warning you, Krieger, don't try to
confuse me."

"I swear—I wasn't."

"You know you've been unbearable."

"I swear—I didn't."

"You haven't once teased me. You haven't
once...grabbed me. For the past two days you'd have
walked on water if I asked you to....." She took a
gulping breath, horrifyingly aware that her eyes were
stinging. "And these are practically the last days I
have with you..." She took another gulping breath,
terrified that feelings were bubbling to the surface that
she couldn't control. "And I wanted those days. I
needed them, Rand, only I need them with you. *You,*
not some paragon of a saint auditioning for knight-
hood!"

"Sweetheart, you seem to be feeling so..." Rand
stopped, waiting for her to fill in the blanks.

"Angry!" So embarrassingly, out-of-control angry that she launched herself at him.

"Yeah," he murmured as he caught her. "Angry."

Leigh thought she was. She swore she thought she was, but a far more dangerous emotion than anger exploded when she touched him. Magic—a right as rain magic—it was always what she felt in his arms. His power and strength, the texture and scent of his skin were as familiar as water and air, but Lord, far more critical to life. At least her life.

His head was already conveniently tilted down, making it just so easy to frame his face between her hands and hold him still. She kissed him once, hard, and discovered it wasn't what she wanted at all. So she kissed him a second time, softer now, testing herself as much as she was testing him. It still wasn't exactly what she wanted, so she tried another. And another.

He'd done it to her a thousand times—offered her cherishing, treasuring kisses, kisses designed to make a woman believe she was the sun and the moon and precious beyond price.

Suddenly there had never been anything more important in her life than to show him the real truth. The giver was always the gift. Rand was the precious one. He was the man to be cherished. He was a woman's treasure. He cast spells, her man. And just this once Leigh wanted to cast a spell for him, weave him a story of how special he was, how desperately wanted, how loved.

She claimed his mouth with her lips, her tongue, swayed deliberately against his hard lean length. Beneath his shirt, her hands stroked the plane of his chest, shifted to knead his shoulder blades and spine. Ruthlessly, tenderly, fiercely, she touched him the way

she'd wanted to before, the way she'd always wanted
to.

Inside, she felt a low coiling ache deep in her ab-
domen, a restless hunger, a building recklessness.
Maybe fear mixed in there, too, because nothing was
simple about loving Rand nor could be. Later she'd
have to pay those prices. She knew that, yet she just
couldn't seem to summon up caution.

Tonight was for him. She'd had the power to please
him before, and never understood or believed it. It was
easy. So easy to love him, to know where and how to
touch, because Rand's response gave her all the an-
swers.

His eye had the dark burn of desire; his arousal
pressed hot and hard against her; his face tautened in
the stark harsh lines of control . . . and his hands. Her
big strong falconer's hands were shaking. He wanted
this. She could have shot herself for not knowing how
much he wanted this, wanted her, needed this, needed
her.

"Leigh . . ." He tore his mouth free from hers and
lifted his head. His voice was thick and strained. "You
have to know, love, what you're asking me for."

"Yes."

"You're sure this is what you want?"

She met his eyes. "Yes."

"You're sure . . . very sure . . . that this is right for
you?"

Something in his gravelly voice made her pause. Her
gaze searched his face. "You used that exact same
phrase before," she said slowly. "On the hillside, the
night of the gypsy festival. You said you wouldn't
break your promise . . . unless you were sure it was right
for me."

"Yes."

"I released you from that promise before. Honestly, Rand, you have a completely unmanageable sense of honor."

A ghost of a smile never reached his eyes. "I'm only asking you to tell me what you feel."

Which she never had. And for such good reason. He'd changed her entire life, opened doors to emotions she never knew existed, altered her feelings about herself as a woman for all time. But Rand could never understand that if she told him, because he had never really met the Leigh Merrick from Stanton, Kansas.

She hesitated, needing to give him what he asked, burdened impossibly by truths she'd left too late to tell him. There seemed only one thing that her man of honor could value more than truth . . . and that was honesty.

She took a breath, and reached behind her. "You want to know how I feel?" There were two hooks and eyes in the middle of her back, then a long zipper. "I feel . . . no regrets, no doubts, no shame . . . for wanting to make love with you. It's not that I'm so sure about what's right or wrong, but . . ." The bodice fell away, exposing her bare breasts. She wished they were perfect for him yet all she saw were flaws. The stays of her formal dress had dented her skin with two red streaks; her nipples were puckered as if she were cold. Or scared. Stubbornly she shagged down the rest of the dress, pushing the long half slip with it, leaving her with nothing but lace-trimmed panties. "But I happen to love you. And loving you makes this right for me. *That's* how I feel, and if it takes seducing you to prove that to you, Rand—"

She was never sure what specific thing she said that triggered the keg of dynamite. She never anticipated how much dynamite she was actually dealing with. She heard the rough, raw sound come out of his throat only seconds before he scooped her up. By the time her spine bounced on the bed, his mouth was covering hers in a kiss as hot and wild as unleashed lightning.

He tugged off his shirt with his mouth still on hers; he unzipped his tux pants and kicked them off without severing the kiss. When he finally let her up for air, her lips stung and ached, and there was a fierce fearsome look in his eyes that made her heart pound. It occurred to her that she was no longer in control of this seduction, that possibly she'd never been in control of this seduction, that all those nights she'd never understood how much her falconer was holding back.

Light and darkness swirled under her closed eyes. The power in Rand flowed over her, inciting reactions and response that she'd never dreamed she was capable of. His mouth was a thief, traveling from throat to breast to thigh, stealing an inch of her soul at a time. His hands stroked, rubbed, tickled, kneaded, until her heart was racing, racing, as though she'd been running a hundred miles an hour.

He was impossibly rough. He was unbearably tender. When he discovered the red marks on her breasts, he laved them with his tongue and growled, "I'm burning that damn dress, Leigh."

She wanted to smile, and never had the chance. He did terrible things to her. Wicked things. Dangerous things that made her feel terrifyingly, awesomely... loved. Civilized layers peeled away. Fire, fueled by countless nights of denial, flamed like a torch in darkness. He already knew what excited her.

He used that knowledge to please and incite and torment until she was burning up and aching. When he finally peeled off the strip of lace on her hips, her arms were wide, open, reaching for him.

She felt the pressure of him, filling her, stretching her, an intrusion of the most intimate kind. There could have been pain, if he hadn't taken such care to prepare her. There would have been shame, if it had been anyone else but Rand.

She met the fierce vulnerable look in his eyes, and felt a yielding inside like the shattering of silk. It seemed there was nothing he wouldn't give her, nothing he wouldn't do to please her. As his soul was bared, so was hers. She belonged to him, with him, and that richness of love she could neither deny him, nor herself.

She wanted his pleasure first.

He wanted hers.

It was their only minor discord. He plunged and withdrew in a rhythm determined to bring her release; she met his driving rhythm with an abandoned wildness to incite his. It was the most loving of wars. Leigh had never thought she could be equal—not as a lover with any man and never with Rand—but she discovered, with him, that she could be stubborn.

And that he was more so. The sweet agony built to a fever pitch until she fused with him, convulsed around him in shocked, stunned, liquid shockwaves. Pleasure was a pale word. This was a crash of ecstasy like a ride on a lightning bolt. She cried out, and so, then, did Rand.

When it was over, she felt weak . . . weak and languid and infused with a dangerous sense of rightness. Rand tried to lift his weight off her. She clutched. The bonding between them had not been irrevocable; it only felt that way. Reality had to return, yet she wanted a moment more when they were this, undeniably, close.

"Sweetheart, I'll crush you," he whispered.

"I don't care."

"Believe me, I'm not going far." Rand kissed her brow, her nose, her lips, and then eased away where he could push away the rumpled spread and pull a sheet over them.

She climbed in the crook of his shoulder and he held her there, blessing her temple and cheeks with more silvery soft kisses. His legs twined with hers; his hard chest cushioned her breasts; his hand drifted soothingly, comfortingly, down the length of her spine.

And then he said, "I love you, Leigh."

Her eyes flew open, focused on his face. She assumed that passion would quench the fire in his blue-eyed gaze. Instead it burned hotter than ever. A velvet fist suddenly squeezed around her heart. "You don't have to say that."

"I've wanted to say it for a long time. But you wouldn't have believed me before, would you?" His fingers scraped back her hair, tangling in that red-shot gold. "I fell in love with a princess who couldn't find her castle. I fell in love with a woman I waltzed with in a dusty ballroom in the dark. I fell in love with a lady who tromped the hills with me and Basta. I fell in love with her passion, and her gutsiness, and her mercurial humor, and her sensitivity...and her giant heart."

The fist squeezed tighter. It wouldn't have shaken her if he'd said pretty words in the heat of passion, or all those nights when the frustration of wanting each other could have color-clouded any words he said. Leigh had the terrible suspicion that was why he hadn't. He'd waited until the claw of desire had passed, because for him they weren't pretty words. For him, they were real, and the full weight of guilt pressed on her chest for all the truths she'd left unsaid. "Rand. Wait—"

He shook his head and leaned over her. "No more waiting, sweetheart. I waited until the eleventh hour as it was—only unlike the jerk in the story, I *knew* you were going to fly off at midnight. No, no, no. You're not going anywhere."

"I just . . . there are things you don't know."

"I know everything that matters." His tone was gruff and rough-soft as he anchored her close again. "That wasn't a sweet goodbye we just shared. It wasn't a thanks-nice-to-know-you courtesy roll in the sack. It was two people being naked together in the way that matters, two people making *love* because they'd die if they didn't. You think I'd ever let you go?"

His thumb stroked the crease between her lips, stopping her from saying anything, his touch as strong as a trembling and his eyes aglow with battling tenderness. "You risked your heart tonight. You were scared as hell, but you did it. You love me, Leigh. That's all I ever had to know, and it wasn't your telling me that mattered. It's what you showed me. Don't deny it."

A lump filled her throat as huge as a well. "I can't deny it," she whispered.

"Close your eyes for me."

"Close my—"

"Just do it, okay?" And when her eyelids fluttered down, he kissed each, more gently than the whisper of wings. "Tomorrow, we'll talk about the tough things. Tomorrow we'll sort through anything you want. But tonight, let's just concentrate on the easy stuff. In your mind, can you picture... a gold band on your finger?"

"Rand—"

"Now don't get tense, don't get anxious. All I'm asking is whether you can picture it."

So she swallowed past the lump in her throat. "Yes."

"See how easy this is? Now... can you picture a couple of little falconers? Brown haired, blue-eyed, running around the hills... can you see them?"

In the fantasy of her mind, in the darkness of her dreams, she'd already imagined Rand's children a thousand times. "Yes."

"Can you picture a bed, love? A plain, innocent old bed. And then picture what I want to do to you in that bed for the next fifty years—"

Her eyes shot up. She didn't, couldn't, answer that question, which didn't seem to bother him at all.

"Tell me you don't want those things, Leigh. Tell me you don't feel just as much in love as I do. Are you going to deny what you want?"

She reached for him and pulled him down, unable to deny him anything he asked. Through the long night, she denied him absolutely nothing at all.

When Rand woke up, midmorning sun streamed through the windows and the bed beside him was empty.

Leigh could have been anywhere from the bathroom, to her own room fetching clothes, to a trek downstairs in search of coffee. She wasn't. From the hollow sick thud in the cavity of his heart muscle, he knew damn well that the woman he was going to marry had panicked. And run.

He was so sure that he grabbed the phone. His first call, to the front desk, revealed that she'd claimed her passport and had a cab called for her. His second call, to the airport, placed her on a flight leaving Vienna in—he checked his watch on the bedside table—four minutes. Paris, New York, then a changeover and direct flight to Topeka, Kansas.

When Rand hung up the phone, he threw himself into the closest chair, well aware that he was strangling mad at her and scared from the gut—yet none of the emotions assaulting him included surprise that his bird had flown.

He'd made a mistake...a mistake that he of all people should never had made. How many dozens of peregrines had he raised to home to him? Yet any falconer knew that however courageous and intelligent and strong the falcon, there was a level where the creature was fragile. You never pushed a falcon who was afraid.

He'd pushed Leigh hard, knowing damn well she was afraid.

Not of him, but of herself. Not of love, because after last night there was no question in his mind that Leigh loved him. Trust, love, respect, honesty—she'd offered them all to him last night, as completely and powerfully as a woman can give a man. So it came down to the fear she'd always had. The fear, at that crushing self-esteem level, of believing in herself, of valuing what she wanted and needed enough to reach for it.

Rand lurched out of the chair and started packing. Unfortunately, he had to go home first. Even temporarily rearranging his life would take a major juggling act. After that, he needed to track down an address from Frau Stehrer—sooner or later Leigh would want her things packed and sent.

And after that, he figured it was past time he had a complete understanding of the spell of fear Leigh lived with.

He planned to pay a little visit to a witch in Kansas.

On the first day of July, Rand drove his rented motor home into Stanton. The temperature was a hundred degrees and still climbing at two in the afternoon. The heat didn't affect him, since the motor home had air, but the look of Leigh's town did.

Bits and pieces fell into place as he drove the streets she had walked most of her life. The town was set in a dusty, sun-drenched corner of the state and surrounded in all directions by miles of cornfields. It wasn't big—maybe a population of ten thousand—but the community values Leigh had grown up with were easy to see. Main Street was suffering with a badly struggling economy, yet there wasn't a drop of litter on the asphalt. The white frame church—clearly the focus of all social activity—had a fresh coat of paint and there wasn't a bar in town. The library was the newest building, not big, but a sign in front listed every family who'd helped put it up. The sign was as big as the door.

Past the business section were rows of residential streets. Most houses were clapboard or frame, painted

white, some huge and rambling, some small and
squat. It was a town that pushed old-fashioned values, and it was definitely a town that valued its kids.
Children were everywhere—playing ball in the streets,
biking and skateboarding, stampeding an ice-cream
truck, and racing through every sprinkler in sight.
There was only one exception.

Rand had the uneasy feeling which house belonged
to the witch before he was halfway down Green Street.
Suddenly the kids and dogs thinned out. A boy on a
bike dipped into the street to avoid riding the stretch
of sidewalk in front of the Silverthorn mailbox. Hers
was the only fenced yard, the only veranda without a
lawn chair or porch swing. In a town full of children's laughter and sunshine and sweat-in-the-heat
life, this house was cemetery quiet and grimly shut-
tered. Big trees that should have provided cooling
shade instead provided gloom; no light would dare
peek through the choke of foliage.

Rand tried to imagine Leigh playing—romping and
stomping and having fun in this house—and couldn't.
He thought of her fragile confidence, her expecta-
tions of rejection, her innocent joy in the simplest
things he took for granted. And his heart started
beating like a trapped slam.

He parked the motor home in the driveway, stepped
out in the baking heat, and walked up the porch of the
veranda. The door was open, but the inside room was
so dark that the screen door revealed nothing of the
room inside. He knocked. Twice.

In his mind's eye, he half expected a seven-foot-tall
abusive-looking battle-ax. He got a five-foot-two
dowager with ramrod-straight posture, severe tufts of
gray hair, glasses thirty years out of style, and long-

sleeved going-to-church clothes in the middle of a
Tuesday afternoon.

"I don't abide salesmen," she said through the
door.

"I'm not selling anything. I'm looking for Matilda
Silverthorn."

"So you're smart enough to read a name on a mailbox. That doesn't cut any mustard with me. State your
business."

"My business is simply talking with you. I'm a
friend of Leigh's. My name is Rand Krieger—"

"*You.*"

He heard surprise, horror, and most definitely en-
mity in that single syllable. She obviously recognized
his name, which told Rand that Leigh had talked
about him...and in a way that obviously displeased
Matilda. Until that moment, he'd had no idea how he
was going to handle the woman. There'd been no way
to formulate a plan until he got a look at her.

The screen door clapped open and he got that good
look at her. She sized him up with one narrow-eyed
glare and then ushered him in, swiftly, not with any
claim to southern hospitality but as if she was praying
no one in the neighborhood had seen him yet—particularly, he guessed, Leigh.

He was instructed to sit in a horsehair chair next to
a table with an open Bible. The room was stifling hot
and dark and smelled of disinfectant. His unwilling
hostess perched at the edge of the opposite chair, her
knees clammed together so tight they had to be sweat-
ing.

"I won't offer you iced tea. You won't be here that
long. And I can't imagine what you think you're do-

ing here, but I can tell you right now— Leigh doesn't want to see you."

Rand had to give her credit for aiming straight for the jugular, yet oddly he felt his antipathy fading against her. What he saw behind those thick-lensed bifocals—and never expected—was fear. He said quietly, "You're sure of that."

"Haven't you done enough? She didn't come back the same, because of you. If you cared about her at all, you wouldn't cause her any more trouble. Besides . . ." Matilda pushed up her glasses. "If she were going to marry anyone, it'll be Joe. He's been after her for years."

"Joe?" Rand noticed she didn't have the nerve to look at that well-thumbed Bible.

"He owns the dry-goods store in town. Fine boy. He fixed my roof, comes in every time I have a leaky faucet, never charges me a dime. She's very fond of him, always has been. If she's going to marry anyone, it'll be Joe. So you might as well clear out before she's seen you."

"Thanks for the advice," Rand said politely. "Now if it's all right with you, let's cut to the chase."

"I beg your pardon?"

"Joe isn't on the map. I am. I've come for Leigh, Ms. Silverthorn, which you figured out the minute you saw me. She's going to give me a helluva battle, but I didn't come here to fight with you. I came here for some straight talk that's never going any further than the two of us."

"I don't understand."

Rand figured she understood just fine. There was only one conceivable reason that she was afraid of him. "I can't tell you that I expect we'll be bosom

buddies, but I promise that you can be honest about
what you need—from Leigh, from us. She's not going to live in Stanton. That's hard for you. How often
you want to come and see us—or how often you want
us here—I'll make sure it works out. You have health
or financial problems, now's the time to lay them out.
The only choice you don't have is to interfere in
Leigh's life in a way that hurts her, because I won't
allow it . . . but nobody's deserting you. If that's what
you've been afraid of—''

It was; he could see it in her expression. The witch
was afraid of having no one, the equation he'd never
factored into the spell she worked on Leigh. All those
years she'd tried to harness Leigh with intimidation
and guilt; all those years she could have had the security of love if she'd just offered it.

Maybe she could change. Rand doubted it; she'd
been swimming in bitter soup for too many years. For
Leigh's sake, and as long as she didn't infect Leigh
with any more of her bitterness, he could afford to be
kind.

It was the princess he needed to get tough with, and
that encounter was still coming. He left the gloomy
house on Green Street and headed for Leigh's place.

Leigh dropped Mary Sue at her house, then Joey at
his. Both kids had begged a ride home from the library, and somehow she'd been suckered into a couple of ice-cream cones en route.

As she backed out of Joey's driveway and headed
down Springtree, she fussed with her car's air condi-
tioning. It was just as temperamental as her nerves.
Since she'd returned home from Austria, it was obvious to Leigh that certain things in her life were never

going to change. She still suckered in for any child in
sight; she still raised cats, and she still got lost five
miles out of Stanton.

Other things, she'd discovered, were irrevocably
different. Back when, she'd never have stood up to her
aunt, much less been bluntly honest with her. Back
when, she'd never had gone to work in a white T-shirt
dress with a gash of red for a belt. Back when, she'd
never have had the courage to mail the letter to Hautberg, Austria, that should have arrived—by her best
guess, yesterday morning.

Her stomach had been in an antsy state of nerves
since—by her best guess—yesterday morning. Maybe
Rand would ignore the letter. Maybe he'd already
written her off. She'd jumped ship. Run out. When a
woman did something that stupid, maybe no expla-
nation or words of love could fill the breech. It
weighed in her heart like a clunk of lead.

She turned off Springtree onto Fielding, her
thoughts distracted when she spotted the huge silver
motor home down the block. It took up a whole
driveway. As she drove closer, she realized it was *her*
driveway the motor home was blocking, forcing her to
park on the street.

Some neighbor obviously had an out-of-town visi-
tor, but they could have had the courtesy to *ask* before using her driveway—she'd get a ticket if she
parked on the street all night. Feeling aggrieved, she
climbed out of her car with her eyes on the big silver
bullet—which was why, for a few seconds, she missed
the man on the shaded steps of her porch, sitting not
only in the impossible heat, but smothered in cats.

Her cats. Worthless, Trouble, and Aggravation were
all aptly named. Trouble, the taffy angora, was draped

on his shoulder; Worthless was belly up on his lap, and
Aggie was wound around his left ankle.

Rand looked so comical, covered in cats, that she
wanted to laugh. Only just then she couldn't, because
she felt a shifting, spinning sensation as if her whole
world was tipping. This time, in the right direction.
For the first time in weeks, that clunk of lead lifted off
her heart.

He looked her over as though he was thirst and she
was water, and he never said hello. He said, "Don't
bother trying to say anything sweet. I'm so mad at you
I can hardly think. If you ever cut out on me again, I
swear I'll lock you in an ivory tower for the rest of
your life."

He didn't look mad. He looked hot and stubborn
and a little itchy with all those cats. He looked dear,
like the breath of air her lungs were starving for, and
she didn't waste time asking how he'd found her. A
long time back, she'd discovered that Rand simply refused to lose anything that mattered to him. "It
looks," she murmured, "like you brought the ivory
tower with you just in case."

He glanced at the motor home. "Good thing, too.
At the time I didn't know we were going to be transporting cats."

"Transporting?"

"Up to Pennsylvania. How else are you going to
meet my family?"

"Your family—"

"You'll need a ring on your finger before we go.
The ring's in the motor home now. So is instant glue,
if you give me any trouble. I'm warning you, Leigh,
I'm in no mood for an argument. I'm staying—in fact,
this thing stays parked right outside your door until

you agree to come with me. I don't care if it takes a
hundred years.''

"Well, hell," Leigh murmured. "Maybe you'd
better show me that ring.''

Rand had never been slow. He lurched off the porch
as if the seat were hot, making cats scatter every which
way. He hustled her inside the cooled motor home
faster than a Vegas dealer could spot a sucker.

It was quite a motor home, with a built-in TV, built-
in stereo system, and most relevant, a built-in double
bed. She noticed the bed, then the two pale pink velvet boxes sitting squat on the dining counter. One box
was small and square, the other narrow and oblong.

Rand locked the door. "To keep the air condition-
ing in.''

"Hmm," she said. She caught his grin, but she saw
the sudden razor-raw look in his eyes, too. So typical
of the man she loved, he used playing as a mask to
hide his vulnerability. He hadn't been so sure of his
reception.

She intended to make him sure, absolutely sure, of
her, but he temporarily diverted her attention when he
opened the ring box. The gold band was simple, not
ornate, which Leigh thought was an unbearable thing
for him to do. Always, she'd known that at the core
her values were basic, not ornate, and his perception
made her eyes well with tears.

"You don't get it until the wedding," he said severely. "But I thought I'd better do something to make
up for being so mean, so you get this one now.''

By then he was opening the oblong box. Inside, on
a nest of velvet, was a long gold chain with a falcon
carved in pure sapphire. Her eyes welled with more

tears. He attached it around her neck, and she could feel his shaky fingers. "You like it?"

"I love them both. I love you. With all my heart." She blinked back the tears and anchored her arms securely around his neck. "I wrote you, Rand. The letter's probably on your desk in Austria. And I need to tell you what was in that letter."

Rand shook his head. "Sweetheart, you don't have to tell me anything." The minute he saw her, he'd guessed that his visit to the witch was superfluous, that Leigh had untangled herself from that old spell on her own. When she spotted him, there'd been a light like a rainbow in her eyes, a steady, sure softness surrounding her like a glow. Leigh belonged with him. She already knew it, and any minute now, his pulse would stop racing. It was just that he'd been living with the fear of losing her for weeks. His heartbeat couldn't seem to remember how to climb down.

Leigh wasn't helping. With her arms still locked around his neck, she shadow-walked him to the back of the motor home. As bedrooms went, this one was tiny. There wasn't room for anything but the double bed and them, and the whole time she was telling him this story about a thirtieth birthday and a wish that turned into a stupid, shallow game.

"I thought I was a fake. That's why I ran. Because I was afraid you fell in love with someone who didn't exist. I never told you I was a librarian. I never told you about the cats. I didn't want you to know—anything—about my real life, because it was so dull, so peanut butter."

She probably kissed him a dozen times, making it extremely difficult for him to listen. He wanted, badly, to listen, because the more he understood this self-esteem thing she battled with, the more he could help her work on it.

"The fear was *real,* Rand. I always knew a leopard couldn't change its spots. No one can really change their basic character. So I thought it was hopeless, because in my heart I thought I'd always be peanut butter and dull and steadfast old Leigh, and no one had ever really wanted steadfast old Leigh...."

She smiled at him, inviting him to share the humor. Nothing was striking him funny just then, not the painful self-image she used to have of herself, nor the dangerous way she was flicking open the tab on her bright red belt. The belt came loose. She tossed it over his shoulder in an abandoned gesture.

"Are you listening to me?" she demanded.

"I'm trying my best." Mostly he was trying to reconcile the cocky distance she'd thrown that belt with the shy, insecure introvert he'd first met. And now she was shaking the pins out of her hair.

"Unfortunately I had to come home—I needed to come back here—to discover that I was wrong. I was so sure I'd automatically revert to being a mouse and a wallflower, but it wasn't that way. Because of you."

He wasn't exactly sure what she was holding him responsible for, but he had a pretty good idea that he was in trouble.

"Maybe people don't essentially change. But what happened to me wasn't about change; it was about *growing.* It was about letting part of myself free that hadn't been free before. Like your peregrines. You don't train them to fly because that's already their instinct. You train them to trust you, Rand, and I just never learned to trust me before—"

Down went the summer-weight panty hose, then up and over her head went the white T-shirt dress. The sapphire falcon bounced, then glittered in the sweet shadow between her breasts. He said, "Honey, you're all through talking."

"But I want you to know that I don't have my head in a fairy tale anymore, Rand. I know what I want. I know what I need—"

She was making that very clear. Another day, he decided, they'd work on her confidence problem.

At the moment he had his arms around her. She felt so good he thought he'd break.

They had the nuts and bolts of a real life to build together. That had nothing to do with fairy tales, which she knew—and so did he. There was no question in Rand's mind, though, that she'd woven a spell around him from the instant he met her. A good spell. The best of all possible spells. An enduring, irrevocable spell of love.

* * * * *

SILHOUETTE® Desire™

COMING NEXT MONTH

#673 BABY ABOARD—Raye Morgan
Carson James was suave, charming and as far from fatherhood as a
man could get. Were Lisa Loring's enticing ways enough to lure him
into marriage...and a baby carriage?

#674 A GALLANT GENTLEMAN—Leslie Davis Guccione
Sailing instructor Kay McCormick had one rule for smooth sailing—
never get involved with club members! But then Jake Bishop and his
daughter guided her into the deep waters of love.

#675 HEART'S EASE—Ashley Summers
Valerie Hepburn's tragic past left her feeling undesirable and
unattractive. But could persistent businessman Christopher Wyatt
persuade Valerie to take a chance on living...and loving?

#676 LINDY AND THE LAW—Karen Leabo
Free-spirited Lindy Shapiro was always getting *into* and *out of*
trouble. But Sheriff Thad Halsey wasn't about to let this beauty
go...not before apprehending her heart.

#677 RED-HOT SATIN—Carole Buck
Hayley Jerome needed a fiancé fast—her mother was on her way to
meet him! Outrageous Nick O'Neill conned his way into playing Mr.
Wrong, but he felt very right.

#678 NOT A MARRYING MAN—Dixie Browning
When a silent five-year-old appeared on November's *Man of the
Month*'s doorstep, secret agent Mac Ford had some questions. But
tracking down beautiful Banner Keaton only added to the mystery.

AVAILABLE NOW: